For Teddy and Ellie

Contents

The Hole / 1
The Wheelbarrow / 5
The Baubles / 8
The Imposter / 13
The Lie / 17
The Teacup / 20
The Casserole / 24
The Pine Cone / 28
The Buoy / 32
The Magic Horse / 37
The Belly / 41
The Auction House / 45
The Widow / 49
The Secret / 54
The Gallows / 58
The Three-Legged Dog / 63
The Puddle / 67
The Queue / 71
The Medicine / 77

The Stag / 82
The Sack / 86
The Gourd / 91
The Rain Barrel / 95
The Café / 99
The Chandelier / 104
The Trick / 107
The Snub / 111
The Ditch / 115
The Quarry / 120
The Stain / 125
The Wolf / 130
The Crossroads / 134
The Giants / 140
The Woodpile / 144
The Emerald / 148
The Outhouse / 153
The Suitors / 157
The Stationery / 162
The Chicken Coop / 166
The Poison Cup / 171
The Roots / 175
The Dancing Soldiers / 179
The Grudge / 184
The Darning Bag / 188
The Statue / 191

The Heat Wave / 195
The Pillow / 200
The Shears / 204
The Locked Room / 208
The Portrait / 212
The Hanged Man / 217
The Glut / 222
The Grapes / 226
The Siren / 231
The Garden / 235
The Trail / 240
The Princess / 243
The Three Lodgers / 248
The Hermit / 254
The Anniversary / 258

The Hole

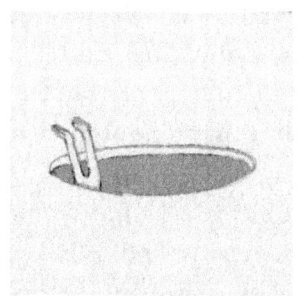

A farmer's calf had gone missing, so he set out to find her.

In a far pasture he discovered a hole he'd never seen before. The hole was perfectly round and wide enough that he couldn't jump across. The farmer was perplexed. No animal could've burrowed so deep or with such precision, and he didn't know how else to explain it.

He assumed the calf had fallen in. Her tracks stopped at the edge of the hole. When the farmer looked down all he could see was darkness, and when he listened all he could hear was the sound of the wind. The air above the hole felt cold. It made his heart race to lean forward.

It was too late to accomplish anything—already the sun was setting. The farmer walked home, thinking about ways to fill the hole and how best to comfort the young cow's mother. If she went looking for her calf she might also fall in, and where would it end? A problem like the hole wouldn't fix itself, the farmer knew.

In the fading light he kept his gaze on the ground.

That night sleep wouldn't come. The farmer tossed and turned in his bed. What if the hole grew larger? What if his son went to explore? The boy could be foolhardy, indulging his every curiosity, no matter his father's instructions. It wouldn't be enough for the farmer to warn him away.

So the farmer went back to the hole. He found his way in the dark, careful not to cross paths with the little people. As he entered the pasture he thought he could hear voices. Men and women were congregating around the hole—some faces he knew and some he did not. He recognized the town veterinarian and the mail carrier. He saw two old maids with their arms entwined and a red-headed man with ears like jug handles.

The farmer wondered if he was dreaming.

"What are you doing here?" he asked no one in particular. "It's not safe."

The people were all carrying things. One by one they approached the hole. The auctioneer cradled an object against his chest. He dropped it over the side, looking relieved, and promptly backed away. The solicitor's wife, who was famous for having five daughters, the eldest of whom had joined her, carried something less heavy. She stood at the hole's edge and turned out her apron.

"Stop!" the farmer shouted. "Can't you see there's no bottom?"

That's when he saw his son. Like everyone else, the boy appeared to be holding something. The farmer felt a sickening weight in his belly. Without thinking, he fought his way forward, clutching and shoving through the scrum. Whatever the boy was holding was invisible to the farmer, concealed by a thicket of arms and torsos. People objected as he passed them, but they were all burdened by possessions of their own.

His son turned. In the moonlight the boy looked elated. He grinned at his father, as if the two were playing a game, and rushed in the opposite direc-

tion, arriving at the hole before the farmer could join him. Whatever he'd been carrying, he threw.
  The farmer exclaimed.
  He didn't pause but dove straight after.

The Wheelbarrow

A man asked to borrow his neighbor's wheelbarrow. It was harvest time and there were more apples than he could carry.

"You can use it," his neighbor said, "but you must bring it inside every night."

The man agreed, thinking his neighbor was concerned it might get stolen. The possibility seemed unlikely. The wheelbarrow was old—its wheel wobbled. Still, the man had a use for it, so he wasn't in a position to judge.

The first night, he remembered to bring the wheelbarrow inside. After he'd delivered the last batch of apples to the packinghouse and had washed his hands with vinegar, he tipped the wheelbarrow against the wall. The wheel would need to be replaced, the man thought, but he was reluctant to make repairs on something he didn't own. Maybe he'd give his neighbor a bottle of cider as a show of gratitude. That would be easier.

On the second night, the man forgot to bring the wheelbarrow inside. He only remembered when he was lying in bed. Because he was still awake, he pulled on his pants and went to move the wheelbarrow. The man was annoyed at his neighbor, though it wasn't his neighbor's fault that he'd forgotten. The man returned the wheelbarrow to the packinghouse and trudged home.

On the third night, it rained so hard that the windows shook. The man didn't forget the wheelbarrow—he made a decision to leave it. He'd intentionally turned it upside down in the orchard. No one would be thieving in such weather, he thought, and the wheelbarrow wouldn't fill with water.

The following morning it was right where he'd left it.

But when he turned it over he gave a terrible scream. Little people had made a home under the wheelbarrow during the night. No human was allowed to see how the little people lived—the shapes of their homes and the precision of their roads. The man wouldn't have been so foolish if only he'd known.

The little people took the man's eyes so he'd never spy again. He could still hear and speak, but he refused to say what had happened. The man's sons let that corner of the orchard grow wild, and within a year they'd abandoned the property altogether. Every turned-up cup on the drying board had become a potential danger. Every hat left on the table could be a new home to the little people.

The man's neighbor never reclaimed his wheelbarrow.

The Baubles

A girl was born with a weak heart. Her skin was pale blue, and her fingers and toes were cold to the touch.

The girl lived in a remote village. There was no medical care, except for the midwife who'd delivered her, and certainly no one qualified to repair the girl's heart. The closest thing to an artisan was the glassmith, who mostly made windows. The glassmith knew the girl's parents, because everyone knew everyone, and he listened with concern when they visited his studio.

"Our daughter needs a new heart," her father said. "Can you make one?"

By now the girl was old enough to sit quietly as the adults spoke. Her lips were purple, the glassmith observed. She wore mittens and a scarf, even though the studio was uncomfortably warm, and still she looked cold.

The glassmith and his guests were surrounded by baubles. These trifles didn't serve any purpose other than being beautiful. They were pink and orange shapes that had visited the glassmith in his dreams. No one had ever asked to buy them, nor was he keen to sell them, though this, he thought, would be a different endeavor—a bauble shaped like a heart.

"Yes," the glassmith said. "I can do it."

And so he did.

First the glassmith studied a pig's heart, which he acquired from the butcher. He was confident that the same number of atria and ventricles would be present in a human heart. Of course the girl would require new and larger hearts as she became older, but this was an opportunity for him to improve his craft. At all times he was aware that her life depended on him.

His only concern was that her heart might

break. Glass was more fragile than flesh and bone. If she was treated poorly, or if she wasn't sufficiently careful, her new heart would be liable to crack, and even the smallest splinter could be fatal. Her final moments would be spent in agony.

"You, more than anyone else, must protect your heart," the glassmith warned her. "To have a long and healthy life, you must be safe."

The first time her heart was damaged was because of a boy. By then the girl was an adolescent, very nearly a young woman. The boy had whispered sweet things to her and proposed a future together, but later his feelings had soured and he'd made rude comments to his friends. When those statements had reached the girl, she'd winced. She'd felt a pain in her chest and had gone to see the glassmith, who'd confirmed that her heart was under abnormal strain.

"Will all boys be cruel?" she asked.

"Cruel?" he replied. "No, but all boys are stupid."

"Then I won't trust my heart to another boy," the girl resolved.

The second time her heart was hurt was because of a girl—a woman, really. By then some years had passed. This woman had loved the girl and valued her, but had found fault with her meekness. She'd demanded a bolder lover. When the girl had failed to meet the woman's expectations, she'd experienced a familiar pain. There'd been a grinding in her chest and she'd gone to see the glassmith, who'd confirmed that her heart was at risk.

"Will all girls be this difficult to please?" she asked.

"I haven't met *all* girls," he said. "At least they're better than boys."

The girl was vexed. "All this time," she complained, "why has no one wished for a normal heart? Not you, not my parents—not even me! If wishes sometimes come true, and people wish for ridiculous things, why not a better solution?"

The glassmith nodded. He looked down at his feet, then up at the ceiling, where his baubles hung like comets in the sky.

"You see my art?" he asked the girl. "Each one came to me in a dream. I woke with a different shape or color in mind and then tried to make it, and each time I failed. Each one is a failure—the wrong color, the wrong shape. It's very frustrating. It makes me want to smash them all to pieces, but I don't. Instead I put them up for people to enjoy."

"That's your explanation?"

"Why wish for a normal heart?" the glassmith mused. "Won't you still feel frustrated?"

The Imposter

A man was arrested for impersonating the prince. His resemblance was uncanny.

The imposter had performed at birthday parties and weddings—dressing in costume, hugging people, and exchanging well-wishes. No one had mistaken him for royalty. Why would the prince be attending a regular person's birthday party? Or a wedding? It didn't make sense.

The prince wanted to see the imposter for himself.

The man was retrieved from the dungeon. He'd been stripped of his clothes when he was arrested, and chained to a wall for days. Someone had the good sense to bathe him, but still the prince wrinkled his nose. The imposter, perhaps sensing an opportunity, also wrinkled his nose—and while it could've been construed that he was mocking the prince, the two looked so alike that the prince guffawed.

"Do me again," he said.

The imposter walked like the prince. He waved like the prince. He copied every gesture the prince made, as if he were staring into a mirror.

The prince was charmed by this performance. Henceforth, he declared, the imposter was to be released from the dungeon and given a room at the palace. The man had broken no laws, the prince said—and while this wasn't strictly true, the laws were changed so that impersonating royalty was no longer a crime.

For a time the prince enjoyed the imposter's company. The two would appear together at state functions, to the confusion of royal guests. The imposter's voice sounded nothing like the prince's—it was deeper and accented—so he rarely spoke aloud, but no one commented on his silence.

Sometimes he would appear without the prince, *as* the prince, without warning or explanation. Only when the imposter yawned could someone see he was missing a tooth.

Eventually the prince tired of his twin. He ordered that he be sent away, but first that his nose be cut off. It was unclear whether the prince had changed his mind about punishing the imposter or was making an example of him, but a person would think twice before pretending to be royalty.

A man without a nose didn't look like anyone at all, only himself.

After he'd been denounced, the imposter joined a road crew. It was the labor he'd performed before impersonating the prince—heating tar in a cauldron and filling potholes, with a kerchief tied around his face to prevent dizziness from the fumes. Four men took turns shoveling tar while a foreman oversaw their efforts. Often, weeks or months had passed since a pothole had been reported. As the road crew collected firewood for the cauldron, someone would inevitably complain about the size of the pothole, how long it had persisted, and how many wheels or axels had been damaged in the meantime.

The foreman would wave over the imposter.

"Don't talk to me," the foreman would say, as the imposter removed his kerchief. "Talk to His Highness."

The Lie

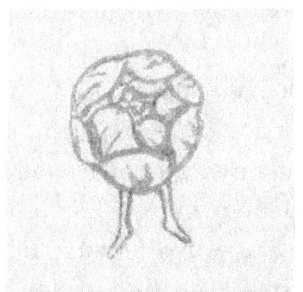

An army was bivouacked on the outskirts of a town. Officers slept in the townspeople's homes, enjoying all the comforts they afforded, while the soldiers camped in tents.

One soldier, tired of sleeping on the ground, claimed to be an officer in order to commandeer a hayloft. The farmer knew what an officer looked like—not this bedraggled person. But the alternative was a confrontation, so the farmer opened his barn, where the soldier slept very well, despite sneezing at the hay.

It was only a small lie, no taller than the soldier's thigh. Nonetheless it hit the ground running. The lie was fleshy, without hair or fur to keep it warm. Some people would describe it as a beef heart. Others said it looked like a cabbage with legs. They all agreed that it ran very quickly, pumping its scrawny arms, and made a hideous, gleeful sound.

The lie spooked the town's animals, particularly the horses and chickens, and caused the dogs to bark. It also scared the townswomen, careening into them while they hung up laundry, or running through open doorways, leaving behind a trail of bloody footprints. The lie ate flower petals and drank from puddles. By the end of the first day, everyone had tired of it.

News of the lie reached the officers. Normally they would've ignored it, ordering the soldiers to decamp for another town, but a rumor had been started—that the lie pertained to the war effort. The officers knew how rumors could affect morale, so they ordered that the lie be caught.

It became the top priority for every soldier.

In no time at all they'd chased the lie up a tree. There it clung to the highest branches, chittering as it rocked in the breeze. None of the soldiers were eager to climb after it. A consensus was reached that the lie would have to come down eventually. The soldiers made a fire and prepared to wait.

Early the next morning they were awoken by a thump. The lie had fallen out of the tree. Some suggested it had been climbing down, or maybe jumping from bough to bough, but the lie had slipped and now was dead.

The soldiers gathered in a circle. There was some discussion about whether or not to bury it. Then one soldier, with red hair and ears like jug handles, kicked dirt on the lie. After that the soldiers wandered off, leaving its body undisturbed, to be a meal for some larger animal.

The Teacup

A woman wished to become pregnant. It was a fairly common wish.

The woman's husband also wanted to be a parent. He'd often imagined himself as a father. He might've wished for a son, he thought, but he would've been equally happy with a daughter—a miniature version of his wife. The woman didn't wish for one or the other. Her wish was for herself, not for her husband or the baby.

Her pregnancy was routine. The woman chewed on ginger root and took long walks, even in stormy weather. When she went into labor she sent for the midwife and banished her husband to the other room. He would've been too anxious during the delivery, she said, to which her husband agreed. The woman and the midwife huddled together like a pair of conspirators and spoke in low voices.

The woman gave birth to a teacup.

It was a very fine teacup—the porcelain was as white as chalk, with a powder-blue filigree. The midwife checked for a saucer and spoon before delivering the afterbirth. People often wished for things without considering the consequences, she thought, and while she tried not to judge, neither was she sympathetic. The midwife's nephew, her sister's child, had once wished to fly. The whole family had watched him float away.

The woman's husband was stunned. The midwife provided him with instructions—what foods would be most nourishing for his wife and how much rest she required—but instead of a son or daughter there was a new cup on the drying board. Many people visited in the following days, some family, some curiosity-seekers. They asked the husband questions he couldn't answer. Would the teacup grow? Could the visitors drink from it? If so, would their wishes also come true?

The woman made no effort to explain herself.

She turned to face the wall and ignored everyone, including her own mother. Each day after their guests had gone home, she refused to touch the teacup. She refused to even look at it. She only spoke when necessary and didn't make room to share the bed, though it could easily fit two. Her husband slept upright at the kitchen table.

Was it strange that he loved the teacup? He'd loved inanimate objects before—a chair made by his father and a stone wall from his childhood. He could remember a time prior to the teacup and, now, a time *after* the teacup, which already felt more rewarding. Every night, while his wife slept, he would gently scrub the porcelain. The man didn't consider himself to be clumsy, but he agonized over dropping the cup. At the same time he knew it was impossible—that he would never lose his grip, no matter how soapy the water. He always admired the filigree before placing the teacup back on the drying board.

Once the woman had healed, she left without warning. Perhaps she'd wished herself away.

The man didn't pursue his wife or send inquiries, because he understood her decision to be final. Why make the situation worse? Perhaps she'd remarry, he thought, or become pregnant again—it wouldn't affect him either way. He continued to care for the teacup. Eventually the curiosity-seekers stopped visiting.

The Casserole

A woman decided to murder her wife. After she'd made the decision, it seemed like a reasonable thing to do.

She decided that poison would be the best way to accomplish her goal. She couldn't imagine strangling her wife or pushing her down the stairs—or she *could* imagine those things, but she didn't think she could do it. There was a vile casserole her wife loved to eat, consisting of noodles, fish, olives, and cheese. Even the dog wouldn't touch it. The woman would serve her wife a fatal meal.

On the night of the attempted murder the woman prepared a salad for herself. Her wife wouldn't be suspicious, she knew, because she often called the casserole disgusting—the taste, the smell, even the sight of it.

"Enjoy," the woman said.

She didn't know where to look as her wife consumed the poison, so she stared at her own plate. But, after a moment had passed in silence, it became clear that her wife wasn't eating.

"Is something wrong?" the woman asked.

"It's just that I had a big lunch and I'm not hungry. I'm sorry—you went to all this trouble. I promise to eat the leftovers."

"No bother," the woman said, doing her best to remain composed. She stuck a forkful of salad into her mouth.

After the failed attempt she wondered if she'd been lucky. If not for her wife's big lunch she would've died, and maybe it would've been a bad thing. Maybe the woman would've grieved for her wife. Maybe she would've been discovered by the country bailiff and hung from the gallows until she, too, was dead.

But that night, when they were lying in bed, her wife got up to pee, accompanied by the dog.

Afterward, she and the dog fell back asleep, but the woman remained awake until dawn. During those long, insomniac hours, her frustration turned into annoyance and her annoyance turned into rage, until she became more convinced than ever that she wanted to murder her wife.

The next day she reheated the casserole.

"Did you use more salt than usual?" her wife asked. She'd only taken one bite, not enough to be lethal or even cause mild distress.

"I don't think so," the woman replied. "Have more."

"It's really very salty—too salty to eat. I'm sorry, my love."

So the woman was forced to throw away the casserole. Maybe her wife had been correct—maybe she'd used too much salt? Or maybe the poison she'd bought had been salty. The woman had no other choice but to make her own poison.

Who knew that murder could be so tedious?

Finally, she was ready to serve her wife a fatal meal a third time. That night at dinner she watched her take a tentative bite, and then another, this one smaller than the first.

"What's the matter now?" she demanded.

"Nothing. It's delicious."

"It's not too salty," the woman said. "There's no salt at all."

"No, it's fine."

"You can't be full from lunch—I watched you. You've barely eaten all day."

"That's just it," her wife said, putting down her fork. "All day long I've been thinking about eggs. What if we had breakfast for dinner—wouldn't that be fun? Eggs, potatoes, and bacon? I'll cook. You've cooked enough."

The woman stared at her unsuspecting wife.

"You know what?" she said. "Enough of this."

The woman grabbed her wife's plate. She forked bite after bite of the casserole into her mouth, trying not to gag while eating, though the smell filled her nose. She must've looked ridiculous, she thought. She felt ridiculous. Her wife laughed. The dog barked and barked.

Then the woman died, and not a moment too soon.

The Pine Cone

An old man's health had been in decline. Finally, on a day like any other day, he died.

The man's daughter, who'd been caring for him, felt both sadness and relief. In the days to follow she thought she recognized his presence elsewhere. Her father had been a regular presence in her life—his absence would take some getting used to. Perhaps, she thought, she'd never get used to it.

First she saw him in the eyes of a donkey. A young boy was leading the animal down the road when it stopped in front of the woman's house. Despite the boy's words of encouragement the donkey refused to move. The woman was in her front yard, tending to her garden. She looked up from the soil and it was like staring into her father's eyes—stubborn and soulful.

Of course it wasn't her father—the woman knew that. Still, it seemed remarkable that the donkey had chosen her yard, on this day, to stop and linger. Whatever the animal was thinking, it didn't say. The woman almost asked the boy if she could give it a hug, but instead she went inside and cried, and when she came back the donkey was gone.

The next time she saw her father she actually *heard* him.

It was a clear day. The woman was in her kitchen, kneading dough, when she was startled by the sound of thunder, so loud and resonant that it couldn't have been anything else. At the same time, the weather was mild. Perhaps there were giants in the distance, she thought, throwing boulders? The sound came again, as loud as before, and struck any doubt from her mind.

The woman went outside to look at the sky, expecting to see storm clouds, but there were none.

"Did you hear thunder?" her neighbor asked.

He was an elderly man, nearly her father's age, who'd also come outside to investigate.

"I thought it might be giants," the woman confessed.

"Me too!"

They both laughed and looked up again. The woman's father had disliked the neighbor. For years he'd accused the man of being a petty thief, with no proof to support his claim.

"I'm sorry for your loss," the neighbor said in a solemn voice.

"Thank you," the woman replied.

"Would you like to come inside for tea?"

The woman accepted her neighbor's invitation. Often, when a person was invited to tea, everything had been arranged in advance—the cups and saucers set out, the tea brewed. However, her neighbor's invitation seemed to have been spontaneous. He busied himself in the kitchen while the woman waited in the living room. She could hear him opening and closing cabinets.

The woman hadn't been inside the neighbor's house before. The man was a widower. His home was tidy, she thought, but it didn't reflect his personality, as if he'd preserved his wife's tastes. She tried to recall how long ago his wife had died. She and her father had brought butter as a gift. It had been a strange thing to bring, the woman now reflected. She felt bad they hadn't been more thoughtful.

"Would you like some cake?" the neighbor called from the kitchen. "I'll only be a minute."

Maybe it was the discomfort of feeling guilty, but the woman suddenly hated her neighbor. Why did he get to live while her father was dead? What gave him the right—what use or purpose? It wasn't fair, she thought. She couldn't eat cake and pretend to be friends. She couldn't even look at his smiling face.

The woman decided to leave.

Before she departed she took a decorative pine cone. She deliberately stole it. Obviously she couldn't display the pine cone in her own home, in case her neighbor came to visit or even looked through the window. She would have to bury it in the ground. She left without saying goodbye, hugging the pine cone to her chest and firmly closing the door behind her.

The Buoy

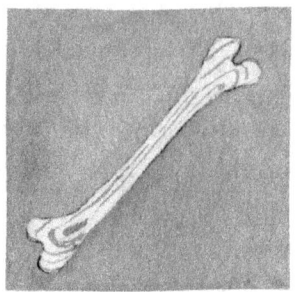

Once there was a boy whose bones were made of wicker. His father was a scarecrow and his mother was not.

The boy's limbs were sturdy as a wicker chair. His ribs were like a picnic basket, with all his organs neatly tucked away. His heart, lungs, liver, and kidneys were all normal. It was only his bones that made him different.

"You must never tell anyone," his mother had cautioned him, "or people will cut you open to see your insides."

So the wicker boy had kept his secret safe.

One day the wicker boy chanced upon two brothers by a lake. The brothers had been arguing, but they fell silent when they saw him approaching. Though one brother was clearly older, both were larger than the wicker boy and each had a menacing disposition.

Their faces turned from scowls to smiles.

"Greetings, chum," the older brother said. "What a stroke of luck! We were looking for a solution and here you come."

"Yes, here you come," the younger brother echoed. "Exactly the person we need."

"You see, my brother and I have a contest—who can swim to the buoy and back the fastest. Do you see, out there on the water?"

The wicker boy looked where the older brother was pointing. Sure enough, he saw a buoy floating on the surface of the lake, not too distant from the shore.

"Can't you decide for yourselves?" the wicker boy asked.

The brothers glanced at each other. Their smiles faltered.

"Impossible," the older brother said.

"Definitely not," the younger brother agreed.

"All you need to do is count while my brother swims to the buoy, then count for me, and then you're on your merry way. How's that sound?"

The wicker boy thought it sounded more complicated than that, but already the brothers were removing their shirts. Some people looked vulnerable in the nude—the brothers only looked larger. The wicker boy felt vaguely exposed, though he remained fully dressed.

"Ready?"

The older brother waded into the water and began to swim. The wicker boy counted in his head. One, two, three, four.

"Here's what I'm thinking," the younger brother said. He addressed the wicker boy, though they were both watching the older brother as he circled the buoy. "When he gets back and you count for me, you'll say I was the fastest—otherwise I'll break your scrawny neck. How's that sound?"

The wicker boy kept his eyes on the water. Like his arms, legs, and ribs, his spine was made of wicker—though, of course, the younger brother didn't know that. In fact the younger brother looked capable of breaking *real* bones.

"What do you say?"

"I'm counting," the wicker boy replied, and so he was. Nine, ten, eleven, twelve.

The older brother returned to the shore, panting. When he stood, the water streamed from his head and shoulders. Almost immediately the younger brother waded into the lake and began to swim.

The wicker boy counted in his head.

"Listen," the older brother said. "When he gets back, you'll say I was the fastest. If you don't, I'll hold your head underwater until you're drowned for good."

Again the wicker boy kept his eyes on the water. It would be difficult for the older brother to submerge his body, he knew—difficult, but not impossible. The wicker boy's skeleton was made from wood and therefore he floated. Still, the older brother looked strong. Surely he could drown the wicker boy if he wanted to.

"Yes?" the older brother confirmed.

"I'm counting," the wicker boy replied. Thirteen, fourteen, fifteen, sixteen.

Finally the younger brother came back. He stood in the shallows, hands on his hips, breathing heavily. Both brothers stared at the wicker boy—one in the water, one on the shore, one faster and the other slower. The wicker boy had no siblings, so he could only guess how important it was to win.

"Well, chum?" the older brother asked. "No more counting."

The wicker boy thought about having his neck snapped. He thought about being drowned. He couldn't think of a way to satisfy both brothers at the same time—maybe if they'd given him longer to scheme, but they'd both swum very fast, faster than he'd expected, and the wicker boy wasn't much of a schemer.

So, instead, he ran.

The wicker boy didn't run over land, where the two brothers could've easily caught him—he ran over the surface of the lake, where they couldn't outpace him, no matter how fast they swam. The wicker boy's feet made splashing sounds as they struck the water, like leaping in puddles. He didn't have a better plan.

The Magic Horse

A woman noticed a spider's web in the corner of her kitchen, too high to reach with a broom. She got a rag and chair and stood to wipe the corner clean.

Once she was standing closer she noticed a small horse caught in the web. The horse was so small that she mistook it for a toy. It made whinnying noises and feeble efforts to kick its legs.

Who could make such a toy? And why would it be here, in the woman's home, where no children ever played?

The woman removed the horse from the spider's web. The tiny creature was warm in her hand. She could feel its heart beating and forgot all about cleaning the web. She carefully climbed down from her chair.

The next day the woman went to the market. She didn't have a stall, because she normally traded eggs and honey with her neighbors, but neither did she intend to stay for very long. She only had one thing to sell.

"Come and see the magic horse!" she announced.

In truth the horse was mostly normal—the only magic thing about it was its size. It ate like a normal horse and shat like a normal horse. It galloped in tiny circles, but it had to be penned or it would run away.

A crowd of shoppers gathered around the woman.

"How much?" someone asked.

The woman was a good bargainer. She'd soon earned a considerable sum of money for herself. Someone else took possession of the horse and the woman went home wealthier than before, thinking she might've earned even more money if she'd made a tiny saddle. An important part of salesmanship, she knew, was presentation.

The next time she checked the spider's web she discovered a very small falcon. The woman spent the rest of the afternoon making a tiny hood, no larger than a thimble. She also made a tiny perch and leash. Like the horse, the falcon was mostly normal except for its size, eating and preening like a normal bird. The woman knew it would fetch a good price.

When she went back to the market there were even more buyers than before. People were enamored with the falcon. They fed it pieces of raw meat, commented on the sharpness of its beak, and complimented the woman on her craftsmanship. No doubt the hood, the perch, and the leash helped her fetch a greater price.

The next time she checked the spider's web she was alarmed to find a man. He was smaller than the horse, but larger than the falcon—which was to say, the normal proportion of man to beast. The woman feared he was one of the little people. She watched him struggle in the web. He tried to address her, but his voice was so faint that she couldn't understand.

The woman took him down and placed him under a teacup. The man pushed from the inside, but he couldn't move the cup, his tiny fists plinking against the porcelain. After a few minutes he stopped struggling.

While she was debating what to do, the woman finally cleaned the spider's web. She would make tiny clothes for the man, she decided. She would make furniture that was just the right size. She wouldn't sell him, but if he *was* one of the little people and they discovered him in the woman's custody, they'd know she'd treated him fairly. When she felt brave enough to remove the teacup she found him slumped on the table—whether from hunger or exhaustion, the woman couldn't say.

From that day forward she kept the tiny man. Over time, with a proper diet, he grew, but not to the size of a normal person. He never stood taller than the woman's knees. The man spoke a foreign tongue. He wouldn't forgive being trapped under the teacup, despite the woman's subsequent care, always glaring at her and grumbling to himself. She never once heard him laugh.

The Belly

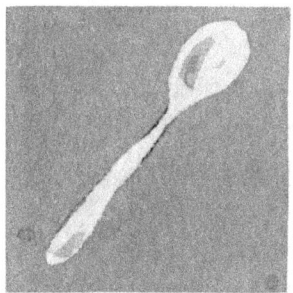

There once was a boy who loved to eat. He loved it so much that he wept whenever his belly was full.

A time always came when he couldn't eat another bite. The boy tried eating smaller portions. He tried arriving at the dinner table sooner and leaving later, after everyone had finished their meal, but nothing could change the outcome.

Every night he wished he could eat without interruption. It would've been rude to wish out loud—people usually kept their wishes to themselves. The boy's father might wish for a new wife, since the boy's mother had died the previous winter. The boy's grandfather might wish for his missing teeth. But the boy only had one wish, which he made unapologetically.

One day, without warning or explanation, his wish came true.

That morning, at breakfast, he began to eat, only noticing with time that he wasn't full—that, bite after bite, he could swallow more. The boy didn't know his wish had come true. He asked for a second helping and a third. His father refused to give him a fourth helping, but the boy didn't mind, so excited was he by the change.

At lunch he also finished a second and third helping, and was refused a fourth time. His belly remained as flat as the floorboards beneath his feet.

That night at dinner, the boy ate with glee. By now he knew his wish had come true. His father and grandfather, who were, of course, familiar with his tears, silently watched him. Something about the boy's joy rankled them.

"How are you doing this?" the boy's father asked.

"I can eat anything I want!"

"Is that so? If you can eat anything you want, then eat my spoon."

"And my napkin," the boy's grandfather said.

The boy didn't know whether it was advisable to eat a napkin and a spoon, but he decided it didn't matter. After they'd passed his lips it wouldn't be his concern. First he ate the spoon, careful not to gag, then he ate the napkin.

"How is this possible?" his father mused.

"I told you—I can eat anything!"

"But I need my spoon. Where did it go?"

The boy shrugged. Helping after helping, bite after bite, he hadn't considered where the food might be going if not to his belly.

"There's only one way to find out," his father said. "You must eat your grandfather. We'll tie a rope around his waist. He can report back what he sees on the other side."

The boy's grandfather was unenthusiastic, but it was the sensible thing to do. A length of rope was found. There was no need to wait until morning, when the boy would be hungry again, since, of course, his belly was never full.

"No biting!" his grandfather insisted. "Don't you bite me!"

"I won't," the boy promised, not wanting to taste the old man's flesh between his teeth.

It took a long time, much longer than eating the napkin and spoon. The boy's father preferred not to watch. He kept leaving and reentering the room. The boy's grandfather was afraid of being suffocated, so he offered himself feetfirst, with his arms thrust over his head.

Finally the deed was done.

"What do you see?" the boy's father hollered.

The old man dangled from the length of rope. As he was lowered from above, he thought the boy's throat looked different from how he'd expected, though, of course, he was no expert. The walls on either side were stained black. The pit below contained the napkin and spoon, amid the detritus of previous meals.

"Wait!" he shouted. "Stop! I know where I am."

But already it was too late.

The boy's grandfather had emerged from the neighbors' chimney and into their fireplace. The whole family was assembled before him—the husband and wife, their three daughters, and a grandmother whom the old man had known since childhood. The neighbors stared at him, twisting on his rope. The old man felt absurd. It was the most undignified thing ever to occur to him, at an age when dignity mattered the most.

The Auction House

A man brought a violin to the auction house. The auction house would sell the violin to a third party and the man would receive payment, from which the auction house would extract a small fee.

People often tried to sell stolen goods. For this reason the auctioneer needed proof of ownership. If he was confident that an item, such as the violin, belonged to a customer, then he would try to sell it. If not, he would alert the country bailiff.

"Do you have proof of ownership?" the auctioneer asked.

The man seemed surprised by this question.

"What do you mean?" he asked.

"A receipt of purchase? Or letter of provenance?"

"I can play," the man said.

That wasn't proof enough—or it was proof of something else, that he could play violin. But, before the auctioneer could say so, the man had begun to demonstrate, notching the violin under his chin and raising the bow. The sound the violin made was extraordinary. Obviously the man deserved credit for his performance, but the instrument's craftsmanship was beyond comparison. The violin even *looked* more beautiful while it was being played—like a little red fox nuzzled against his chest.

The auctioneer felt conflicted. It was true that, in the past, he'd sold items whose ownership had been dubious. In those instances he'd told himself that he wasn't committing a crime—he was merely an auctioneer whose job it was to bring buyers and sellers together.

The man finished his song.

"I'll take it," the auctioneer said. "But keep the bow."

The man left with money in his pocket and

went directly to a café. It was a warm evening so he sat outside, at a table with two chairs, and ordered a bottle of wine. When the waitress brought two glasses he said he only needed one. She'd also brought a menu, which she left in front of him.

As the man was filling his glass a dog came to sit by his feet. The dog was small and white with a dignified snout. He didn't wear a collar, but his coat was clean, suggesting he belonged to someone.

The dog looked at the man.

"Hello," the man said. "Can I help you?"

The dog didn't reply, but waited attentively.

"Would you like some wine?"

The man took a saucer from an adjacent table. He placed it on the ground and poured a little wine. The dog lapped it up. When he raised his face his snout had been stained red, if only temporarily.

"You'll want to eat something," the man said with a chuckle, "or else you'll get drunk."

When the waitress came again he ordered soup and bread, but asked for the bread first. A moment later she returned with a fresh loaf. The man broke the bread into chunks and fed them, one at a time, to the dog. The man didn't butter the bread and he needn't have bothered—the dog ate with a ravenous appetite.

"More wine?" the man asked.

The evening was still warm, though the sun was setting, and the tables around him had been filled. The man volunteered his unused chair to a group of three—two men and a woman. They thanked him and gave a quizzical look to the dog.

When the waitress came back the man asked for more bread.

"I'm sorry, sir," she said. "If you're ordering for your pet I'm supposed to ask you to leave."

"What if it's for me? I haven't had my soup yet."

"I'm supposed to ask you anyway."

There was laughter from the other table—the man suspected he was the reason. The waitress looked apologetic, but it wasn't her fault, he thought. She was just doing her job. He smiled to show he wasn't upset. The man picked up his bow from under the table, and also picked up the dog, which, at his touch, became a white violin. The other diners gasped in disbelief. The man notched the instrument under his chin and started to play.

The Widow

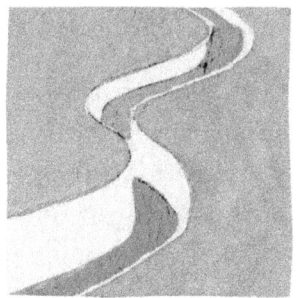

A widow had become seriously ill. She was so weak that she couldn't get out of bed.

"Children," she said, "you must work together until I'm better. Life waits for no one."

"Yes, mother," the eldest daughter replied. "Don't worry—we'll take care of everything."

First the vegetable garden needed tending. If someone didn't pull the weeds they would choke the carefully maintained rows. This chore was assigned to the youngest daughter, who had the least concern for getting her clothes dirty.

Unfortunately pulling weeds made her hands hurt. Most of the plants had sharp leaves or thorns, which scratched the poor girl, while others left their roots in the soil. The youngest child had newfound respect for their mother's hard work, but it didn't stop her from complaining.

"I'd rather have no food at all," the girl muttered.

Next the family's clothes needed to be boiled. If someone didn't stew their garments in hot water, fleas would spread from person to person. This chore was assigned to the middle daughter, who had the strongest arms and was best able to stir the cauldron.

Unfortunately the steam caused her eyes to water and her scalp to itch. Fleas that leaped free had to be crushed underfoot. The middle child also gained newfound respect for their mother's hard work, and she also complained to herself.

"I'd rather walk around naked," she said.

Finally the dead needed to be grieved. This chore was assigned to the eldest daughter, who was the most mature and had the most detailed memories.

The girl wasn't sure how to grieve—she'd never observed anyone doing it before—but she assumed it required privacy. She left the family home and went to a secluded place where the trees closed around her.

The girl tried to summon tears.

She failed at first to notice the soldier. His red hair was short, like all soldiers, in order to prevent lice. Unlike other soldiers, he had big ears. Though he was standing at a respectful distance, he and the eldest daughter were still very much alone.

"Hello," the soldier said. "What are you doing?"

The girl considered her response. In truth she wasn't doing anything, just sitting on the ground and attempting to cry.

"I'm mourning the dead," she said.

"Like that?"

"Is there a better way?"

The soldier scratched his jaw. She noticed his shirt was loose around his torso and his pants had been belted with a length of rope.

"Whenever I mourn I try to get low," he said. "Low to the ground, I mean, so the dead can hear me."

The girl remembered how hard her sisters had worked—how difficult and unpleasant their chores had been. It made sense that grieving would require some labor.

"Can I make a suggestion?" the soldier asked.

"Before you make a hole, maybe you could *find* somewhere low—a burrow or an uprooted tree. It takes a long time to dig a grave."

This also made sense to the girl. Together she and the soldier looked for somewhere low, maintaining a comfortable space between them, though she already felt safer in his company. When they found a creek bed with steep walls he offered to lower her down. The walls were higher than she could reach.

"Before you start," he said, "if it's not rude to ask, who are you mourning?"

"My father," the girl said. Then she added, "And *his* father and his father's father, I suppose."

"Which way is home?"

"Back the way we came."

The soldier left her there, in the creek bed, and walked to the family home. Upon arriving he ate every vegetable in the garden rows—all the tomatoes, all the beans, even the unripened gourds. It seemed impossible for one man to consume so much. Next he took the laundry that was hanging up to dry. The children's clothes shouldn't have fit him, but he was terribly gaunt.

As he stole, the other daughters watched him through the window. They whispered to their mother what he was doing, but she was too delirious to help.

The Secret

A woman kissed her neighbor's wife—or that's what he would've said, *his* wife.

The woman was a jeweler. She made earrings and necklaces and sold them at the market, occasionally trading for rare stones. She'd had a number of lovers over the years, men as well as women, though she'd never married. She was discreet and unashamed. She believed that her neighbor was a boor—and a bore—but she was too tactful to say anything.

The woman's secret was long and silky. It lazed around the house, especially when it found a patch of sunlight. It devoured any food she put down, though the woman couldn't tell which end had a mouth, or whether it had more than one mouth. She might not see her secret for days and would forget it was there until she noticed it atop a tall bookcase or curled under her bed.

One day her secret escaped.

The woman wouldn't have noticed, but she'd slept with her window open and awoke feeling unsettled. She tried calling for her secret. She tried putting food in every room and checking its favorite hiding places. The secret hadn't been outside before, for obvious reasons, though it tensed whenever birds or squirrels approached the window. Maybe it had chased one, the woman thought.

She had to find it.

Where to look, with the whole world to choose from? The woman decided to visit the market. She left her window open in case her secret came back, though she expected it was too late for that.

At the market, vendors were arranging their booths, as the woman would've done on a normal day. There were fruits and vegetables for sale, spices, and cookware. People ate baked goods as they strolled the aisles. The woman kept her gaze down. She'd stepped on her secret once before, by accident, provoking the most hair-raising shriek.

It would be a terrible surprise for someone—if, indeed, her secret were there.

She saw her neighbor bargaining with the metalsmith, and, by his side, the neighbor's wife. The two women made eye contact. If anyone could help the woman, it was the neighbor's wife, but the woman was hesitant to ask. Presumably, the neighbor's wife had done a better job keeping *her* secret—and, anyway, something had changed since their kiss. As quickly as they'd looked at each other they looked away, and it was then that the woman saw it.

Her secret was on display among a vendor's scarves. It was sunning itself. Someone only needed to reach for the wrong color and her secret would be revealed.

The woman sidestepped another customer and pretended to finger the fabrics. Her secret recoiled from her touch. She glanced right and left, to see if they'd been noticed, then grabbed her secret and yanked more forcefully.

Luckily for her, everyone was soon distracted.

The metalsmith had crafted a boy from tin, copper, and other alloys, and this simulacrum had crushed her neighbor's hand. The flesh-and-blood man howled in pain. Meanwhile the metal boy was unaware of what he'd done. He didn't know his own strength. He admired this person kneeling before him, his head bowed and his legs splayed, and how their fingers had become entwined. The man's hand had been pulped—pretty shades of pink and red. The tighter the metal boy squeezed, the more it leaked through his grasp.

The Gallows

Three siblings wanted to go to the spring fair. The annual gathering attracted people from all over the region.

"You may go," their mother said, "but remember to hold hands or else you'll become separated."

All the children agreed—the youngest child, the middle child, and the oldest child.

On the day of the fair they set out early. They walked in a line, from the youngest to the oldest, holding hands. The sky was clear, though the road was muddy with puddles. As the children made their way, they talked about their expectations.

"I want to pet the baby animals," the youngest child said.

"I want to eat fried dough," the middle child said.

"I want to see the gallows," the oldest child said.

Because they were holding hands, they could only walk as fast as the slowest child. This required the oldest sibling to take shorter strides, while the youngest sibling had to trot to keep up. Between them, the middle sibling could feel his arms being pulled in either direction.

The closer they got to the fairgrounds, the more people shared the road with them.

The oldest child began to feel self-conscious, but when she tried to let go of her siblings' hands, the middle child wouldn't allow it.

"No," he said. "We promised."

The youngest child also felt constrained. She wanted to pick wildflowers growing by the side of the road. But when she tried to let go of her siblings' hands, the middle child wouldn't allow it.

"If we let go, we'll become separated," he said.

Finally they came to the fairgrounds. There

were more people in attendance than the siblings had ever seen before. There were baby animals to pet, fried dough to eat, and, at the center of it all, a newly erected gallows. A carpenter was still driving in the final nails.

"Piglets!" the youngest child shrieked.

She was so excited by a pen of baby pigs that she pushed through the crowd and vanished from sight. The middle child was aghast. He tugged on his older sister, attempting to follow her, but found it difficult to make a path.

"We have to stay together," he said, turning heads. "We promised!"

The oldest child, feeling embarrassed, took this opportunity to drop her sibling's hand. While the middle child tried to advance, his sister walked backward until she too had vanished into the crowd. When the middle child turned around, she was no longer there.

The boy stopped in his tracks.

"Where did you go?" he asked. "Does anyone see my sisters?"

But, all around him, people had their own children to manage.

It was a long day filled with surprises and delights. The youngest child didn't pet the piglets, but she met a baby goat, six baby ducks, and a miniature horse. Meanwhile the oldest child joined some children her own age. They loitered on the edge of the fairgrounds and laughed at their parents' behavior. There was a boy who paid special attention to her. She thought he might kiss her, but then he left with his father and mother.

Once the sun had dipped low in the sky, the youngest and oldest siblings found each other again. They had forgotten to eat and were tempted by the smell of fried dough. They looked for their brother among the departing families. When they failed to see him they agreed he'd probably left hours earlier. Together they walked home, hand in hand, as their mother had instructed.

The middle child hadn't left. Instead he'd searched for his siblings, clutching strangers and turning them by the shoulder, until he'd been accosted by the country bailiff, with his long arms and legs and his too-tall hat.

"What's the meaning of this?" the bailiff had asked.

"I have to find my sisters."

"Maybe so, or maybe you're a thief. They often claim to be lost children to gain sympathy."

"But it's true," the middle child had protested.

"If you're really looking for your sisters, they must be looking for you. Come with me. We'll wait together."

So the bailiff had brought the middle child to the gallows, where a holding pen had been constructed, just like the pen for the baby pigs. Here the bailiff had detained other fairgoers who were guilty of lewd behavior.

Convicted felons also awaited their sentencing, as part of the day's entertainment.

The middle child had waited for his siblings, but they'd never come. As the afternoon had become evening and the crowd had gotten drunker, the hangings had begun.

The Three-Legged Dog

A man forgot his son's birthday. The next day, when he realized his mistake, he went to buy a gift.

The man approached the local dog breeder. He thought his son might enjoy having a pet, even though he'd never asked for one, because what child doesn't like a dog? The breeder had many different options to choose from, which, the man assumed, meant some dogs would be cheaper than others.

The man saw a three-legged dog playing with the rest of its litter.

"Is it less for that one?" he asked. "If so, I'll take it."

"That dog isn't for sale," the breeder replied.

"What do you mean it's not for sale? Why show it to me, then?"

"I keep all my dogs together, even the ones that are mine."

"What makes it special?

The breeder refused to explain. Maybe the dog was fearless, the man thought, despite its size—maybe it had lost its leg fighting a giant. Or maybe something more valuable would grow from its missing limb. The more the man thought about it, the more convinced he became that the breeder was hiding the three-legged dog in plain sight and hoping it would go unnoticed.

So when the breeder went to make coffee, the man stole the dog. It was easy to carry, not because of anything it lacked but because of its good nature. The three-legged dog kept licking the man's face. He also left the gate open, allowing the other, more curious dogs to explore, so the breeder would think his prize had escaped.

That night the man chained the dog in the front yard, where it howled and cried. No matter how often he yanked on the dog's chain it refused to be silenced. Finally the man's son convinced him to bring the dog inside.

"As long as it stays in your room," the man said. "It's your dog, after all. If it pees on anything, it's your problem—understand? Its mistakes are your mistakes."

The boy agreed, hugging the dog around the neck. Looking at them—his son sitting on the floor, the dog wagging its tail—the man felt foolish for ever having thought there was something special about the mutt. Clearly it hadn't fought a giant. But at least the three-legged dog had been free, and it would be another year before his son's next birthday.

The man put them both out of mind.

The boy brought the dog to his room and closed the door. He placed the dog on his bed, but the dog jumped down. He lifted the dog again, but the dog jumped down and sat at the boy's feet.

"There is a river," the three-legged dog said, "running under your house. Can you hear it?"

The boy cocked his head and listened.

"I don't know," he said. "How does it sound?"

"The water rushes so fast—faster than you can imagine. It cuts through ancient stone. It uproots even the largest trees and carries them downstream."

"I saw a river like that once," the boy said.

"No, you didn't. Every day this river runs higher, under towns and villages. Where will you be when it overflows? When it floods its banks and everything gets swept away, where will you be?"

"Somewhere far from here," the boy said.

"Then we must go."

And so they did. The boy and his dog left that night, but not before the dog had peed on the rug, which the boy not only allowed but encouraged.

The Puddle

It rained all day and into the night.

The next morning, when the boy awoke, he could hear water dripping from the eaves and knew that the storm had passed. He hurried outside to jump in the puddles before his mother could assign him chores.

Already the new day was smudged. The air was loud with the buzzing of insects. The boy jumped from puddle to puddle, trying to avoid worms, and spooked the birds standing in the middle of the road. It felt as if the storm had left something behind—like when a guest visited, the boy thought, and hung an unfamiliar coat by the door.

By late morning most of the puddles were gone. Some had soaked into the earth while others had evaporated into the air. Their hollow bottoms were as dry as baked clay. There was one puddle left, at the base of a large tree, but when the boy approached a crow spoke to him.

"Not that one," the crow said.

"Why not?" the boy asked.

"That puddle isn't for jumping."

Before the boy could ask further questions, the crow had flown away.

The boy stared at the puddle. There was something different about this one, he thought. Aside from being the only puddle, it appeared to be undiminished, as large and deep as the storm had left it. The edge of the puddle was perfectly round.

The boy intended to jump in the puddle to spite the bird, but he was prevented by a nervous feeling. The puddle seemed to be waiting. Anything that waited must also possess patience, the boy thought. He decided to go home to start his chores.

The next day he went to see the puddle again. The boy had dreamed during the night. He'd dreamed the puddle was a frozen pond and that he, the boy, was skating across it. Now, in real life, he thought the puddle appeared to be unchanged, no bigger or smaller than the day before. The boy looked up at the tree, but he didn't see the crow.

As he came closer he noticed something new. The puddle *was* different from before—it reflected the light differently. A hard, opaque layer had formed on the surface, almost like ice, though it was too warm for water to freeze. The boy kicked a pebble and watched it skitter across.

The boy approached. He looked down.

There was no reflection. Or rather, the boy wasn't reflected in the puddle. Looking at the surface he could see the tree above him, its branches and leaves, and the clouds in the sky moving from right to left. Everything was represented in tones of silver and gray, like the world at midnight, except for the boy himself. He waved one hand, then both hands, and made faces. It was as if the puddle had refused to see him.

In his frustration he considered stomping on the surface, but then he thought better.

That night the boy dreamed again. He dreamed the puddle had filled a rock quarry. The boy jumped from a great height and broke through the surface of the water, sinking deeper and deeper, but he never reached the bottom.

In the morning the puddle had attracted someone new—a man with short, red hair and ears like jug handles. The man was crouched under the tree. He glanced at the boy and beckoned him over.

"I know," the boy said, joining him. "The crow said—"

The man tugged on his arm, pulling him down.

"Can you see your face?" he asked. "I don't see my face."

"I know," the boy repeated.

"It makes no sense."

The man let go. He patted the ground until he found what he was looking for—a sizeable stone to break the surface. The boy backed away. He wondered if he'd ever stopped dreaming.

"Please don't," he begged, but the man ignored him.

The Queue

Only when the king was very old did he worry about having an heir, which made sense, since younger men were rarely concerned about their legacies.

The king had never married, but it was easy to find a wife. He gave a command and, within days, a dozen candidates had been gathered. The king voiced his preference and the two were wed.

The queen understood her situation perfectly well. After all, she was a realist. To marry and have children were normal expectations for a woman, and what better situation could the queen hope for? The king might've felt indifferent toward her, but he wasn't unkind. The queen became pregnant right away, which was a relief, and gave birth to a healthy son, which was also a relief.

The prince satisfied everyone's needs. But no one taught him how to behave, not his father and not his mother.

The prince went to visit the queen after the king had died. Technically his mother was still royalty, though she showed no interest in ruling the country. She lived alone and worked at a nearby bakery, despite her allowance from the royal treasury.

"Is there anything to eat?" the prince asked.

"I brought some scones from work. You can have one of those."

The prince eyed the pastries. He didn't know what he was in the mood for, but it wasn't those.

"I wish you'd come back to the palace," he said.

It was a funny word to use—wish. Most people had to be careful what they wished for, lest their wishes come true. The prince couldn't remember wishing for anything in his life. He could *make* the queen return, he knew. He could throw her in the dungeon if necessary.

"I know, dear," she said, sweeping the floor.

"But Roger needs me at the bakery—it's our busy season. We have three wedding cakes for Friday."

"I can send the royal chef. He can make a hundred cakes."

The queen paused in her cleaning. She put a hand on her son's arm.

"You can't always get what you want," she said. "That's life. Go be the best prince you can be."

Outside, a general was waiting for the prince. He'd brought a hundred troops with them, more than were necessary for the prince's safety but fewer than he'd requested. The prince had hoped to impress his mother with the size of his retinue. Now her neighbors stood in their front yards, observing the soldiers with curiosity.

"Send men to the bakery," the prince ordered the general. "Burn it to the ground. If you see a person named Roger, throw him in the dungeon."

On their way back to the palace the prince passed a line of people waiting for water. There was a well at the center of town—everyone took a turn lowering and raising the bucket. The prince and his retinue were a welcome distraction for those who idled.

"What's all this about?" the prince asked his general.

"It's a queue, Your Highness" the general replied. "It has a beginning and an end. When the person in front is served, the next person moves forward, then the next person, until everyone's had a turn."

The prince hadn't waited in line before. As with wishing, he was unfamiliar with the need. Dismounting from his horse, he approached the largest person he could find. His soldiers hurried to flank him.

"You," the prince said. "What do you want?"

The large man looked at the soldiers. He was no fool, despite what people assumed based on his size.

"We're waiting for water," the man said.

"But you're big—why not take it? You can walk to the front and help yourself."

The man glanced at the people on either side of him, but they avoided eye contact. He cleared his throat.

"That wouldn't be fair," he said.

"To whom?"

"To the others."

"Do they need water more than you do?"

"No," the man stammered. "Maybe, I don't know."

"So the person who arrives first gets water first, whether or not he's the strongest or most in need. That seems disorganized to me. It seems to me that people should get water based on merit. Otherwise a big fellow like yourself gets treated the same as everyone else."

The prince was pleased with his reasoning. He happily grunted to himself. Meanwhile the line had continued to move forward, which gave the impression he was addressing someone new — an elderly woman with a glass eye, who smiled and curtsied.

"But I was here first."

"Who said that?" the prince asked.

He and his soldiers moved down the line. The large man, briefly spared the prince's attention, was now staring at his feet. To his right, a normal-sized man faced the retinue. His defining characteristic was a beard.

"I did, Your Highness," the bearded man said.

"What exactly did you mean?"

"I was here before him," he replied, indicating the larger man. "If he wanted water so badly he could've gotten here sooner. The same goes for all of them — they could've gotten here sooner, but they didn't."

"So you think you deserve it more?"

"I was here first," the bearded man said again and thrust out his chin. It was unclear whether he meant to defy the prince or the rest of the line.

"What's your name?"

"Roger."

The prince grinned. Behind him the general shook his head.

"Roger!" the prince echoed. "What a happy coincidence."

The Medicine

A child went to bed complaining of a sore throat and woke the following morning with a fever. She'd sweated through her sheets during the night.

After changing her bedclothes and applying a compress to her forehead, the child's mother retrieved a bottle of medicine. The bottle was brown—so dark, it was impossible to see the contents. Everyone in the family took the same medicine when they were unwell. The child couldn't remember where the medicine had come from or when, but the bottle belonged to her earliest memories.

"Drink this," her mother said.

She measured a spoonful. The flavor would be vile—the child remembered that too. No matter how swollen her throat was, no matter how stuffed her nose, the taste would be worse than any sickness. Even her parents gagged as they swallowed it down.

The child puckered her lips, but her mother insisted.

"Yes, yes," she said, "I know. Very terrible."

By eveningtime the girl was feeling improved. By the next morning she was fully cured.

"What's in the medicine?" the child asked.

Her mother seemed confused by the question. She'd already returned the brown bottle to the root cellar, where she'd shelved it for future use.

"It's just medicine," her mother said.

"Yes, but what are the ingredients?"

"Only good things."

The child was unsatisfied with this answer.

She'd been thinking about the dosage—how they all took one spoonful, regardless of who was bigger or smaller. Wasn't that strange, the girl thought, when her father was twice her size? How could their bodies be so different, but similar in that regard?

"What would happen if we took more?" the girl asked.

The girl's mother gave an impatient sigh. She put a cheek to her brow, then held her at arm's length.

"You're well again," she said. "Stop asking so many questions."

The child resolved to learn for herself.

She decided to conduct an experiment. A subject would take two spoonfuls of the medicine, or four spoonfuls, or however many spoonfuls were required. Obviously, as the experimenter, the girl couldn't also be the subject or she couldn't document the results. What if she fell asleep for a hundred years? Or turned into smoke? She considered dosing the family dog but worried about the differences between animals and humans.

Finally she approached a neighbor child who was younger than she. The two weren't friends, but neither were they unfriendly.

"I'm conducting an experiment," the girl said. "Would you like to be a part of it?"

The boy nodded. He didn't ask for details, which suited the girl just fine. She'd already retrieved the brown bottle from the root cellar.

"You have to drink this," she said.

"All right. But I need your help too."

The boy turned away. He began to follow the stone wall that divided their properties. The girl was irked by this delay, but, at the same time, the boy hadn't asked what was in the bottle or how much he was expected to drink, both questions she preferred not to answer. It was easier to satisfy his request than to explain herself, the girl assumed.

They walked and walked. Sometimes the girl felt confident they were on her family's land and other times she knew for a fact they were on his family's land. She wondered where the boy was taking her. She wished she'd brought the bottle. If so, she could've dosed him when they arrived, far from the eyes of his or her parents.

At long last they came to a tree.

The girl had never seen anything like it before, not even in her dreams. Instead of leaves, hands grew from the tree's branches. They were all different sizes—lined palms and smooth palms. Most of the hands had five fingers, but some had three or four. They were different colors too—red, yellow, and green. The hands became agitated when the boy stepped close. They opened and closed, clenching fists, and made a sound like applause. The hands only relaxed when he stepped back again.

"Look," the boy said, and pointed.

Up high in the branches was a barnyard cat. To the girl's eyes the cat appeared to be unhappy with its situation. She wondered how it had gotten there.

"You see?" the boy asked, his gaze raised. "I'll help you and you help me. But you first."

The Stag

A woman went downstairs in the middle of the night to discover a full-grown stag in her living room. She assumed the creature was awake, because it was standing upright, but the stag remained motionless. Its antlers grazed the ceiling.

The woman hurried back upstairs.

"There's a stag," she hissed at her husband, who was still asleep.

"What?"

"Wake up! Do something!"

The man got to his feet. Yawning, he went downstairs, where he too saw the stag and gave a yelp of surprise.

This noise seemed to animate the beast. With its antlers, it gored their furniture, puncturing cushions and pillows. It gouged deep troughs in the ceiling and walls. Tables and chairs were shoved aside. Window panes were shattered.

The man rushed back upstairs.

"What's happening?" the woman asked.

"There's a stag!"

"I know that! How did it get here?"

The man was dumbfounded. He'd only been awake for a minute. Luckily, he thought, the stag was too large to climb the stairs.

"I'll open the front door," he said. "Then it'll go away."

"Are you sure?"

The man wasn't sure of anything.

He crept back downstairs. He couldn't remember whether stags had good eyesight or not, like giants, who were practically blind. He didn't know anything about stags, except that this one was especially large. The stag was kicking the wall that separated the living room from the kitchen, extending its rear legs over and over again, lowering its head each time. The man was able to reach the front door unseen.

As soon as he turned the knob, a second stag appeared.

The second stag was smaller than the first, but equally agitated, striking its hoofs against the floor. The man was forced back inside. He retreated, pursued by the second stag, who seemed intent to follow him. However, the stairs represented a challenge. The animal tested its balance, moving cautiously, while the man ran ahead.

"Out the window!" he yelled to his wife. "Escape that way!"

So together they climbed out the window.

They found themselves outside. The drop to the ground had appeared to be perilous, but neither of them was injured by the fall, though they were cold in their bedclothes and bare feet. From inside the house they could hear the sounds of destruction. Occasionally a stag would pass in front of a window, like it was a house for stags and not for people, and they would feel as if they were peeping.

"Whoever will believe that this happened?" the woman asked, sounding dazed.

"Whoever needs to believe," the man replied, "except us?"

He was right, the woman thought. She took her husband's hand and gave it a squeeze.

The Sack

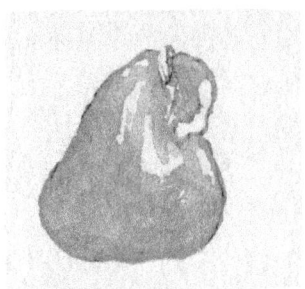

A young girl was sitting by the crossroads. At her feet was an empty sack. When a man came along, it was unclear whether she was waiting for someone else or only resting her feet.

"Little girl," he said, "are you all right? Do you need any help?"

"It's my sack," she replied. "It's too heavy for me."

"I'm going south," the man volunteered. "If we're traveling the same direction I'd be happy to carry it for you."

"Would you? That would be so kind."

The man smiled. He picked up the girl's sack, which, to his surprise, was extremely light. He didn't understand how it could be too heavy for her, but she was young and slight, and it seemed rude to inquire. Anyhow he was pleased to do something heroic.

As they walked the sack became heavier. The man first felt it in his hands and wrists. Then he felt it in his legs and back. He was perplexed. Nothing had been added to the sack in the short time they'd been together. Perhaps he was already tired, he thought, and the sack had aggrieved his muscles.

"Little girl," he said. "I'm sorry, but I don't think I can carry your sack any farther. I wish I could be more help."

"You were perfect," the girl said.

Then she put him in her sack.

Next a wagon came along, piloted by an old mare. Riding in the wagon was a farmer. He pulled on the reins when he saw the girl sitting by the crossroads.

"Little girl," he said, "why are you all by yourself?"

"I was on my way home, but my sack is too heavy."

The farmer looked at the sack. He looked

down the road.

"Well," he said. "We're going north, to market. You can ride along if you want. Just throw your sack in the back."

The girl did as he'd suggested, but soon the wagon became too heavy. The axles were grinding under the extra weight and the mare was straining against her harness. The farmer pulled on the reins again. He was deeply confused.

"I'm sorry," he said. "But if I don't rest my horse I'm afraid she's going to hurt herself."

"I understand," the girl said. "Don't worry—you were perfect."

She put the farmer, the wagon, and the mare in her sack.

The girl was back at the crossroads when a metal boy approached her. This curious person had been crafted from tin, copper, and other alloys, but he spoke and behaved like a normal child.

"Hello," the metal boy said. "Are you waiting for someone?"

"I've been trying all day to get home," the girl answered. "But my sack is too heavy and now it's getting dark."

It was true—the sun was falling below the trees. Soon it would be nighttime, when the little people traveled the same roads and made examples of anyone they encountered. The metal boy considered the sack, which appeared to be empty, and then considered the girl.

"I can carry it for you," he offered.

So the two began to walk. The metal boy noticed the sack becoming heavier. It had to be so, because the metal boy's arms never tired. He didn't have muscles like a normal boy, or aches and pains like a normal boy.

Soon it became so heavy that he imagined he was carrying an anchor. The metal boy had seen one before in the metalsmith's studio—a giant anchor crafted for a galleon. A wagon and four horses had been required to deliver it. The metal boy had wanted to go too. He'd wanted to see open water. Now he wondered if the sack might rip his arms off his body. If so, *he* would look like an anchor, two legs and a torso.

The metal boy imagined himself being dragged across the ocean floor. He imagined coral and brightly colored fish. He didn't know where these ideas had come from. Had he invented them? Or did they belong to the sack?

"You're perfect," the girl said. "Do you know that?"

"Yes," he said, "I do."

The Gourd

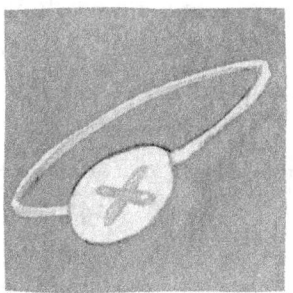

An old man roasted a gourd for supper. When he split the gourd in two he was surprised to find a half dozen geese.

The geese spilled out, one by one. Later the old man would marvel at how they'd fit, but just then he was too surprised to feel anything, even hunger. He waved his arms and shouted, urging the geese outside.

Perhaps he'd expected the geese to fly away. Instead they honked and stomped on his flowers, tapping their beaks against his window. The old man couldn't think straight for all the commotion they made. He opened his door again and the geese marched inside, one by one.

There were exactly six of them—the old man counted. The geese followed him wherever he went, walking all in a row. They honked at the dairy cows. They hissed at the village children. The old man had never been popular before, but now he was famous for his gaggle.

People assumed he had a way with animals so they came to him with questions. Why did a certain goat refuse to stand up? Why had a mare turned sullen? The old man didn't have answers, but he was happy to guess, and sometimes his guesses were correct.

People stopped consulting the village veterinarian. It didn't matter that the veterinarian had more knowledge in the ways of animals. Once people stopped asking, all his learning became useless.

The veterinarian had a wife and child. His family needed to eat, so he became a soldier instead.

As a member of the prince's army the veterinarian traveled far and wide. He carried a weapon for the first time in his life. He fell in love with another soldier, who'd been a butcher before he enlisted. It seemed that every soldier had done something different—farmers, teachers, pharmacists. The butcher had also left a family, like the veterinarian, with whom he hoped to be reunited, but those lives felt remote to them. In every town they passed they saw men and women who reminded them of their former selves, but they didn't know whether to feel envious or sad.

"You see how she doesn't wash her hands?" the butcher said in one town, referring to a waitress at a café. "She'll get sick. They'll blame the little people, but it could've been prevented."

The butcher had an uncanny ability to say who would die next, which, rather than making him popular among the other soldiers, got him shunned. He had one brown eye and one blue eye. His blue eye could see the future, he said.

"I wished to see the future," he told the veterinarian, "and one day my wish came true, but only in one eye."

"And the other eye?"

"It sees what you see. It's confusing to open them both. That's how I recognized you. First I saw you with my blue eye, then my brown eye."

"What else do you see?" the veterinarian asked.

"You're the last good thing I saw."

So the veterinarian made an eye patch for the butcher, which he could wear over either eye depending on his preference. The veterinarian didn't ask what would happen next, because he considered it rude to do so, and when the butcher was killed, the veterinarian assumed he'd wanted it that way.

The Rain Barrel

A man noticed a strange smell coming from his rain barrel. He assumed an animal had fallen inside and drowned.

It would've been easy to remove the corpse, perhaps a rat or an opossum, but what if it was a little person? The man didn't want to be blamed for their death. That was how small problems became big problems.

Whatever had died soon began to fester. The man's family couldn't use the rainwater for cooking or bathing, even if they boiled it, and the nearest well belonged to his neighbor. The best thing to do, the man decided, was to roll the barrel away from his home to where he could empty it. If the little people found the corpse, they wouldn't know the cause of death, and the man could still salvage his property.

So one morning he rolled the barrel down the lane toward the main road. The rain barrel was nearly full—he could hear the water sloshing inside, as well as the corpse bumping against the surface. The smell was even more noxious than before. The man was forced to breathe through his mouth.

Upon reaching the main road he paused to rest. Rolling the rain barrel had been harder work than he'd expected. The man was about to conclude his business when he saw the country bailiff walking his way. The official was unmistakable, even from a distance, with his long arms and legs and his too-tall hat.

"Hello," the bailiff greeted him. "What a handsome barrel. May I ask where you're taking it?"

Reluctantly the man described his situation—the rainwater, the foul smell, the little people.

"Quite a predicament," the bailiff agreed. "Of course, you can't empty it here."

The man considered arguing, but the law was against him. If only he'd arrived at the intersection a short time earlier, he thought, he could've been headed home already. The man told the bailiff he was just resting. Soon, he said, he would continue along the main road, rolling his rain barrel.

"Then we can walk together," the bailiff suggested. "I'm also traveling that direction."

So the two continued on their way, walking side by side.

The bailiff didn't make conversation, which suited the man fine. As the road extended away from his home and twisted upward, gravity weighed against the rain barrel. The task of rolling it became increasingly difficult. Inside, the water lapped and the corpse stank. The man labored under a hot sun.

When they finally reached the summit he paused again to rest. No sooner had he stopped than the country bailiff spoke.

"Of course," he said, "you can't empty it here."

The man nodded to indicate he knew better. He was just catching his breath, he said. In fact he wouldn't be offended if the bailiff went ahead, since he was probably needed elsewhere, but the official only smiled. The man closed his eyes. He nearly wished he were alone, but he caught himself. What if his wish came true and the bailiff disappeared? Surely he'd come back, in a month or a year, and the man would be held responsible. He might even be sent to the gallows.

Once his breathing had returned to normal he continued pushing the barrel.

Now the road sloped away from him and the rain barrel required less encouragement. The man was grateful for the reversal, but only for a short time, as he soon began to trot, and then to jog, while the barrel outpaced him. It wobbled and bounced on the uneven terrain. The man had terrible visions—of the hoops warping and the staves breaking, and his rain barrel being smashed to pieces. The man was running so fast he felt like falling. Would there never be an end to this hill?

He imagined the bailiff behind him, looking down. No matter how hard he tried, he couldn't imagine the other man helping.

The Café

A woman opened a café in a small town. The café was also small, with only three tables, each of which sat two chairs.

The woman had long wanted to run a restaurant. In her imagination it would be a place for artists and intellectuals to meet. She knew she was a decent cook at best, so she hired a chef. The woman would pour wine, brew coffee, and, most importantly, handle receipts. Perhaps one day she'd hire a waitress.

Then the little people got involved.

She never learned why they came. Maybe she'd left a window open. Maybe they had already been there—the café had formerly been a bakery, popular for its wedding cakes. The woman's grandmother had told stories about the little people, claiming they were wicked, but the woman wasn't intimidated. She wouldn't surrender her ambition.

First the little people stole all her spoons. They took the soup spoons, the teaspoons, even the dessert spoons. The woman tried to solve this problem by bringing spoons from home, but the little people stole those too. Now she had no spoons anywhere.

"I'll order more," she said. "In the meantime, no soup—only salads."

"What happens when they steal the forks?" the chef asked.

"Then you'll make sandwiches."

"The secret to a great sandwich is great bread," he confided in her. "We'll make our own."

The chef was different from the other candidates she'd interviewed for the job. They'd all been men, but only the chef had been polite. The others had interrupted the woman when she'd spoken and had generally ignored her questions, implying that she required their approval and not the other way around. One candidate had even patted her on the head. The woman had politely removed his hand. After he was gone she'd screamed into a napkin.

Next the little people stole her salt.

They didn't take it all at once, just a bit at a time. That suggested they were using it, the chef said, which was a good thing. There could be enough for everyone! But the woman refused to share. Though she wouldn't admit it, their salt was more expensive than regular salt because of an ill-advised purchase she'd made. A vendor had touted *his* salt as being superior and the woman had been persuaded. The little people had exposed her mistake.

"I'll protect it," she said.

The chef didn't like this idea—he was concerned for her safety. What if she accidentally saw the little people? They might cut out her tongue, and for what? Surely her health was more important than some salt, he said.

But it wasn't the chef's decision to make, nor had the woman asked for his opinion. She would spend the night. Because she didn't want her tongue cut out, she would wear a bucket over her head. She'd sit on the floor and hold a knife, hoping her presence would be enough to scare them away. There were other restaurants in town, she said—other kitchens with less expensive salt, unless the little people preferred hers, in which case she was out of luck.

On the first night, the chef left early. He didn't stay as the woman was counting receipts because he didn't want to argue. Worse yet, she might try to convince him to stay. The chef went home. He expected to find his daughter asleep and his husband in bed, reading, so he was surprised to discover both them in the bathroom, very much awake.

"What's going on?" he asked.

"We're painting," his daughter said. She was nude, kneeling in the bathtub, and covered in paint.

"It's easier to clean when she's right there," his husband said.

The chef admired the scene. He didn't ask why they were painting after bedtime. He looked at his daughter, working with quiet determination, and his husband, tired but serene, and felt that peace had been restored. This was the center of the chef's world, not the café. The woman and the little people would be there tomorrow.

"I'll make bread," he said.

"And coffee," his husband requested. "Pretty please."

The chef bent down to give him a kiss.

"And coffee."

The Chandelier

A woman inherited a chandelier from her great aunt, a woman she could barely recall. She'd never visited her house before, where the chandelier had previously hung.

"What use is a chandelier?" the woman's husband complained. "We'd be better off selling it. At least then we'd have the money."

"It's made of glass, you idiot," she said. "Anyway, I don't want to sell it—it's mine."

The woman hung the chandelier in their bedroom. Their house was small, with only enough room for the couple and their infant daughter. It hadn't been built with a chandelier in mind.

"I can't sleep like this!" the woman's husband protested. "It's practically touching my nose. What if I sit up too fast?"

So the woman took down the chandelier. That night she lay in the dark, the mattress sagging underneath her, and listened to her husband snore.

The next day she hung the chandelier in their daughter's bedroom. The child was delighted by the jewels, particularly how they refracted the light and shaped rainbows. She obviously preferred the chandelier to her other mobile, the woman noted with pleasure.

But again her husband objected.

"Have you lost your mind?" he said. "What if she grabs it, like she grabs at everything? One tug is all it would take. You might as well kill her yourself."

So the woman took down the chandelier, but neither she nor her daughter was happy about it. The child refused to nap and the woman bounced her too hard on her lap, humming a song about a teacup.

Finally she hung the chandelier over their meal table. Despite her earlier efforts, the woman had to admit it looked best there. Now their guests would be impressed when they dined with the family.

"I can't eat like this," her husband objected. "It's right in my face—I'll go blind from staring at it. And who will clean it when food gets in the chains? Take it down."

But the woman didn't take it down.

Instead she removed three small jewels from the chandelier and cooked them into her husband's food. The shards of glass turned his bowels to lace. First he complained of stomach pains, then he shat blood, and within a week her husband was dead.

"An allergic reaction," the woman practiced saying, as her daughter cooed at the prisms on the wall.

The Trick

A man and his dog had a magic trick. The man didn't consider himself to be a magician—he only performed the one trick.

The dog was small, as small as the man's wrist. Every evening the two of them would go for a walk while other people were outside—to enjoy the light, to meet their neighbors, and to dry the day's sweat. It was then that the man and his dog would perform their trick.

The man had never used a leash. His dog was well-behaved and popular with children. When it was time the man would utter a command and the dog would run away. Then she'd stop, sit, and wait for the second command. Those who knew the trick would also wait. The man would speak loud enough for everyone to hear.

"Come!" he'd shout.

The dog would run toward him at full speed. Meanwhile the man would kneel and open his coat. When she was close enough the dog would leap off the ground, into the man's embrace, and there she'd disappear.

The man would close his coat. Immediately he'd be swarmed by children. They would check his legs and torso, under his coat and inside his pockets, but the dog would remain absent.

After a minute or two had passed, the man would shoo the children away. He'd kneel again, open his coat, and the dog would emerge, happily barking and licking his face. The crowd would applaud, the children loudest of all. No one knew how the trick was accomplished, including the man, who cleaned gutters for a living.

One day the trick failed him.

It was eveningtime. The man and his dog went for a walk, as usual, with the intention of performing their trick, as usual. The man was feeling hot under his coat, which was too heavy for the weather, but he knew it was necessary. Real magicians had props, whether cloaks or hats, to aid their illusions. A prop made a magician *look* like a magician. Still, the man was uncomfortable. Everyone looked so happy in their short sleeves.

The dog seemed to notice his discomfort. When the man issued his first command she tilted her head. Perhaps he should've been concerned, but the man wanted to take off his coat, which he couldn't do until he'd completed the trick, so he issued his command in a sterner voice. Now the dog obeyed. As soon as she was far enough away he called her back, opening his coat for her to jump inside.

Usually the man welcomed the swarm of children. He would laugh as they rudely explored his body, but, on this particular evening, the man didn't laugh. He was patient for as long as he was able and then he shrugged off his coat, throwing it to the ground. The children continued their search, though there was nothing to be discovered. The magic had already occurred. The dog had vanished.

The man enjoyed the breeze. He closed his eyes.

Perhaps, had he opened his eyes, he would've seen his dog falling from the sky. From how high, nobody could later agree. As high as a building, some people said. Even higher, others claimed—from as high as the clouds. In truth, no one had been looking up, because everyone had been looking down at the coat. It was only when the dog landed on the man that their attention was diverted.

The dog had grown accustomed to applause. Now she barked and licked the man's face, but nobody clapped, only gasped or shouted. The children ran back to their parents as the man staggered to his feet. No one offered to retrieve his coat for him. No one seemed eager to touch it.

The Snub

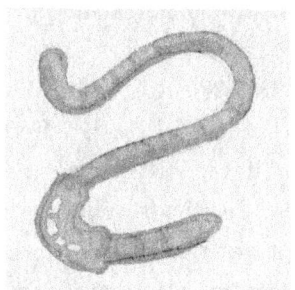

Two sisters had been estranged for a long time—so long, in fact, that they couldn't agree how long.

When the younger sister became engaged she didn't invite her older sister to the wedding, a snub that resonated throughout the town. The younger sister personally delivered each of her invitations. She walked from house to house, carrying a basket filled with envelopes, and knocked on every door. When she came to her sister's house she paused at the gate. Whether or not the older sister was home, witnesses observed the younger sister continuing on her way with undelivered envelopes, so that no one could claim she'd made a mistake.

The younger sister planned to marry the town's undertaker, a tall man who stooped in the presence of others. The undertaker made every effort to treat people with respect. It had been his desire to invite the older sister to the wedding, even if she might decline, though, on this matter, he'd deferred to his bride-to-be. He appreciated that not everyone could be satisfied all the time, including himself. He still bowed when he crossed paths with the older sister, who ignored him.

The older sister was the more reclusive of the pair. As the town's laundress, she was known to everyone but had few friends. People made assumptions about her—that she was lonely, that she was humorless. She would've been a source of more gossip if she'd lived a more interesting life.

So it came as a surprise when she announced *her* engagement.

"A worm?" the younger sister exclaimed. "She's going to marry a worm?"

"It can't be a real worm," the undertaker replied, trying to soothe her.

But it was a real worm—the older sister would show anyone who asked. She carried her groomto-be in her apron pocket. The older sister's wedding date was the day before her sister's ceremony. She hadn't bothered with invitations, trusting that rumor would travel more swiftly than mail, and she'd been correct. Within hours the whole town knew.

"She's only doing it to punish me," the younger sister complained.

"But am I the joke?" the undertaker asked.

"What do you mean?"

"Is the worm supposed to be me?"

The younger sister was too annoyed to disagree. Deep down she knew she'd provoked her sister, but she hadn't expected a public rebuke. The more she thought about it, the more she considered herself to be the victim. Her sister was being petty, she decided. Worse than that—she was jealous.

The undertaker also had hurt feelings. It was true that he was pale and spent much of his time digging in the soil, but was it fair to compare him to a worm? Hadn't he always bowed to the older sister? How could a person bow without legs, a waist, and a spine?

And what about the worm?

The worm had learned that too much attention was never a good thing. It preferred to hide in the older sister's apron than be subject to the townspeople's scrutiny. Under their gaze it was reminded of its worst day, when it had been cut in two. The skies had rained for weeks. The ground had been more mud than dirt—more puddle, even, than mud. The worm had nearly drowned, so finally it had tunneled to the surface, where a bird had been waiting.

The bird had cleaved the worm in two. It had survived the ordeal—or, rather, one half had survived and lived long enough to meet the older sister, to whom it was now engaged. It wasn't such a bad thing, the worm thought, being engaged. Certainly it wasn't the worst thing. But the worm recalled the feeling of being exposed. How many times could it be cut in half before there was nothing left?

The Ditch

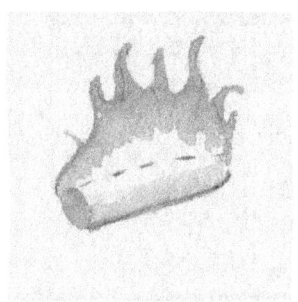

A boy discovered a severed penis in a ditch. The cut was clean, suggesting an especially sharp pair of shears.

The boy played with the penis all day long. He swung the appendage over his head and threw it as far as he could. He compared the penis to his own, though they could've been different organs, as varied as his thumb and his big toe. He tried chewing it. The texture was rubbery and flavorless, which disappointed the boy. He ran his tongue over his teeth and spat in the dust.

It wasn't the first time he'd found something in the ditch. Once he'd found women's clothing. He'd found dead birds, in various states of decay, and a locked sea chest. The boy hadn't been able to move the chest by himself and it had been gone the following day. Nothing stayed in the ditch for long. The boy assumed the little people came at night, but he was never brave enough to wait and see.

When it was time for dinner the boy brought the penis home.

He successfully concealed the penis from his mother, but he was betrayed by the family dog, who whined and pawed at the boy's lap. When the boy's mother saw what he was hiding she shook her head.

"A person doesn't leave a perfectly good penis behind," she said. "Someone will come looking for it. You'll see."

The boy knew it would be easier to lie than to change her mind.

So, after dinner, before it got dark, he announced that he was returning the penis to the ditch. The family dog tried to accompany him, but the boy was still sore. He yelled at the dog until it sulked off. The boy went far enough that he couldn't be seen from the house, and there he sat, watching his shadow grow longer, until he deemed that enough time had passed. He tucked the penis into his pants waist and later slept with it under his pillow. That night he dreamed of the sea chest.

In the morning the penis was gone.

The boy was confused until he went outside and found the appendage in the dog's mouth. The animal thought they were playing a game. He wagged his tail and prepared to run. The boy was moments away from kicking the dog when his mother came outside. She was also upset by what she found—that the boy had lied. He had to think fast if he wanted to avoid punishment.

"I swear I took it," he said. "I threw it in the ditch, I swear. It must've come back by itself."

The woman turned pale. Too late, the boy realized he'd said something he shouldn't have. Muttering to herself, his mother went inside and promptly reemerged with a jar of lamp oil. The family dog, reacting to the tautness in her voice, dropped its prize at her feet.

Before the boy could lie again his mother had set fire to the penis.

The penis burned without complication. Its scant hairs frizzled. Its puckered skin turned smooth as glass and its sutures popped, one by one. There was no odor, like there'd been no taste, though it did produce a thick smoke.

The boy watched in silence. When the penis had been reduced to little more than ashes his mother stomped it out.

The next day he went back to the ditch. He didn't have anything to play with, nor could he think of anything to do, aside from throwing rocks. He tossed a dozen of these, but there was no appeal. Eventually the boy lay on his back, at the bottom of the ditch, and stared at the sky.

He fell asleep.

The boy awoke to a pawing sound. Sitting up, he rubbed his eyes. He couldn't locate the source of the noise, but when he peered across the road he saw a man with red hair and big ears in the opposite ditch. The man was pacing back and forth. The boy experienced a feeling of guilt. It was just like his mother had said—someone had come to retrieve the penis, quite possibly the original owner, not knowing it had been destroyed.

"Hey," the boy said. "What are you looking for?"

The man paused. He faced the boy—his upper half visible above the road. The man looked frantic.

"You've seen it, haven't you?" he asked. "Where is it?"

The boy was suddenly afraid. He scampered to his feet and ran home. He didn't think he was being followed, but he didn't slow down until he met his dog, who mistakenly believed they were playing another game. The animal trotted alongside him, barking and nipping at the boy's heels, with a generosity of spirit that was undeserved.

The Quarry

Over time a quarry had filled with rainwater. The resulting lake was cold and deep.

A single fish lived in the quarry. He didn't know whether he'd been born there or, like the rain, had arrived by accident. Hardly a day passed without something falling in the water. The fish placed these things into two categories—objects that floated to the top and objects that sank to the bottom.

People liked to jump in the lake. They landed with a splash, kicked their legs, and created many tiny bubbles. Sometimes they would jump two at a time, holding hands. The swimmers exited the water as soon as they got in.

They also threw rocks in the lake. The fish assumed the rocks had been thrown, though they could've fallen in by themselves. Rocks made a smaller splash. They caused fewer bubbles and quickly sank to the bottom. Sometimes the fish followed them down, to see where they came to rest.

Only the fish could swim both ways—up and down. For that reason, he believed, the lake belonged to him.

One day a woman jumped in the lake. Or maybe she was thrown—later the fish would consider that possibility. She entered the water like everyone else, with a great splash, but she didn't kick her legs. In fact she didn't make any effort to swim. She sank below the surface, her arms stretched wide, until she reached a particular depth, where she stopped.

The fish cautiously approached her. As he swam closer, he saw bubbles escaping from the woman's lips. Even more bubbles clung to her hair, which floated in a great, complicated mass. The fish lingered in front of her face. The woman opened her eyes and looked at him, and he panicked, swimming away as fast as he could.

The next day she was in the same place. She hadn't moved up or down.

"Excuse me," the fish said, venturing near. "Can I help you?"

"Help me do what?" the woman replied.

"Most people swim to the surface. Do you know how?"

"I can swim—you don't have to teach me."

"It's just that most people swim to the surface," the fish repeated.

"You want me to leave, is that it?"

The fish *did* want the woman to leave. The lake felt uncomfortably small when he was forced to share it with a person. However, he didn't want to be rude. He had very little experience speaking with people.

"Can you kick your legs?" he asked.

"If I want to."

"But you don't want to?"

The woman didn't answer. She pretended to be preoccupied with her hair.

"Can you wave your arms?"

"Mind your own business. I'll go when I'm ready."

The fish swam away to consider his options.

The next day he approached her again. The woman's eyes were closed, which meant, he assumed, she was either thinking or sleeping. It didn't matter to the fish. If the woman refused to swim he'd decided he would sink her. Things either went up or down. Only the fish could occupy the middle.

The fish was unable to speak, even if he'd wanted to, because he was carrying a stone in his mouth. It wasn't a large stone, because he didn't have a large mouth, but it was big enough to provide some heft. While the woman floated with her arms outstretched the fish located a fold in her dress. He spat out the stone and went back for another.

Upon his return, he saw that the woman had opened her eyes.

"What are you doing?" she asked.

The fish couldn't reply while carrying the stone. Even when he'd added it to his previous haul, he didn't answer her, instead going back for another.

"Am I sinking?" the woman asked when he came back.

She appeared to be lopsided. The fish found a fold on the other side of her dress and deposited a stone there.

"What is that? What did you put in my pocket?"

"A diamond," he said.

"Really?"

"There are diamonds at the bottom of the lake."

The woman seemed pleased by this statement, as he'd assumed she would be, but then she frowned.

"Doesn't it hurt your mouth?"

The fish considered her question. It was true, the stones were uncomfortable to carry. Each one was a different size and shape, requiring more or less space, but they mostly felt the same.

"Should it?" he asked.

"Diamonds are sharp. Are you sure it's not something else?"

She tried to catch his eye without moving her head, as her hair continued to swirl around her face. The fish could feel her gaze. The truth was, he'd never seen a diamond before.

The Stain

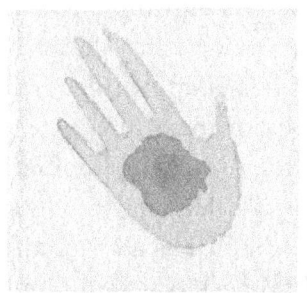

The prince wanted a new robe for his birthday. A red robe, he said, the color of blood.

The task fell to a local merchant. First he had to choose a material that was appropriate for royalty. Next he had to tailor the robe—too big or too small would make the prince look ridiculous. But none of it mattered if he got the color wrong.

Luckily red was an easy color to fabricate. The merchant and his apprentice made a special batch of dye, to be used only once, and treated the royal robe. They agreed that the color was spectacular—a red so deep it flirted with being purple.

The merchant presented the prince with his robe before his actual birthday. That way the prince could wear it to the festivities. The presentation was a minor ceremony including the prince, one of his advisors, and the merchant, who'd left his apprentice back at the studio. The boy had sulked about not being included, stirring the dye with obvious annoyance.

"Perfect," the prince said, holding up the robe to confirm its size. He smiled as he brought the material to his cheek. His advisor also smiled. The merchant did his best to appear humble.

The prince handed back the robe.

"Now make it red," he said.

"Of course, Your Highness," the merchant replied, despite feeling confused. He briefly caught the advisor's eye, but she revealed nothing, ushering the prince to his next audience.

In the courtyard the merchant examined the robe again. Its color was undeniable, he thought, but there were many different shades of red. Perhaps the prince had meant a reddish-pink? Or a reddish-orange? The merchant regretted that he hadn't asked for clarification. He'd have to trust his instincts.

Upon returning to his studio he made a second batch of dye. This new color was many things—bright, playful—but it was certainly red. Though the merchant was reluctant to admit it, he preferred his second effort to his first. In fact he was so proud that he brought his apprentice to share his success.

As he had before, the prince held up the robe to inspect it. Like before, he smiled as he examined the details, then handed it back to the merchant.

"Not red enough?" the merchant guessed.

"Or maybe even too red," the prince said.

The merchant's apprentice nearly objected. Sensing this, the merchant delivered a pinch to his waist.

"Too red or not enough." The prince shrugged, unable to decide. "I'm sure you'll figure it out."

As they left the prince's company the apprentice grumbled to himself.

"He's crazy," the apprentice said.

"Not crazy," the merchant corrected him. "Powerful."

The two returned to the studio with no idea how to proceed. The prince's birthday was mere days away. They had nothing to give him and no inspiration—until that night, when the merchant received a vision. It woke him from a deep sleep and he, in turn, woke his apprentice.

"It's not the dye," the merchant explained. "It's the material—we're not soaking it long enough."

Normally the apprentice would submerge a garment using a long pole. In the merchant's dream he'd *massaged* the dye into the fabric. Of course this would require putting his hands in the solution, plunging his arms as deep as the elbows.

"Isn't that dangerous?" the apprentice asked.

"No more than failure," the merchant said. "I'm sure you'll be fine."

So they treated the third robe as the merchant had described and the result was extraordinary—a color they'd never seen before. The dye also stained the apprentice's skin. Though he washed his hands with lye his palms remained a deep crimson, no matter how many times he scrubbed.

At the prince's birthday festivities they presented his gift.

"Yes!" the prince exclaimed. "That's the color I wanted!"

The other guests applauded. Grasping the apprentice by the wrists, the prince turned the boy's hands palm-up. The apprentice was too surprised to object. He looked at the merchant, who discreetly hid his own hands behind his back.

"You mean his skin, Your Highness?"

"Yes—I can have it?"

"Of course you may," the merchant agreed. "His Highness can have anything he pleases."

The apprentice was removed by the guards, with no objection from the merchant. The prince's advisor took possession of the robe and the next guest presented his gift—a framed portrait of the prince. His likeness was even more handsome than in real life.

The Wolf

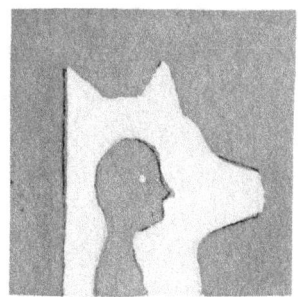

Once there was a boy who turned into a wolf.

It happened overnight, as most changes do. He fell asleep a boy and awoke as a wolf. He barely had time to stretch before the shouting began. No one in the boy's family recognized him—not his brother, not his mother or father. They all thought he was a wild animal. Later, when they couldn't find the boy, they'd assume the wolf had eaten him.

He tried to say his brother's name, but a wolf's throat is different from a boy's throat. Instead of speaking, he snarled, a low and satisfying sound. The wolf-boy dashed from room to room, dodging projectiles, until he escaped through an open door. At the time he gave no thought to what he was leaving behind. He ran to the forest, where he immediately felt calmer.

His first day as a wolf was wonderful. The boy had never fully experienced the forest. Prior to being a wolf, he'd only seen light and shadows and had heard the occasional birdsong, but now he was aware of all the living creatures around him, great and small. He snapped his jaws and ate a butterfly. He investigated the scent of a bear. When night came and the boy grew tired he slept in a hollow tree, as warm and cozy as his human bed.

Even his dreams were wolf dreams.

There were other wolves too. The boy had heard them before, howling. His brother had said they were singing, but now the boy could understand their language, how the wolves were announcing strange disturbances. When he roused himself on the second day he discovered them around his tree.

"Who are you?" one of them asked.

"Who are you?" the boy echoed.

"Where did you come from?"

"Where did *you* come from?"

The boy didn't mean to be difficult—he was still learning how to speak like a wolf. Each new word in the wolves' language replaced an old word in the human language, just like a pocket could only hold so many things. Even the notion of a pocket was gone from his mind. Wolves didn't keep anything longer than they could chew and swallow it.

Every new thing he learned required him to forget something old. Over time the boy forgot his brother's name. He forgot how they'd shared a bed and would sleep head-to-toes, an excuse to knee each other in the back. He forgot which of his parents he'd liked more and why. The boy forgot about being a boy in order to become a wolf. He couldn't be both at once, except maybe in his dreams, where he could remember a particular feeling—like riding on his father's shoulders.

And then, one day, the boy who'd turned into a wolf turned back into a boy, but not the same person as before. He was older and taller now. He awoke in his hollow tree, feeling cramped and cold, and crawled forth. The other wolves snarled at him and the boy ran away. He didn't run home—he didn't remember a home—but in the direction he was being herded. He couldn't communicate with the other wolves because he couldn't speak their language, but he knew, if they caught him, they would tear him to pieces.

Eventually the boy found a new home with a new family. He couldn't explain to them where he'd come from and he didn't stay for long, because, by now, he was almost a man. Many years had passed since the boy had turned into a wolf. He decided to become a soldier. After so many changes he was angry. He wanted an excuse to hurt people.

The Crossroads

A metalsmith crafted a child from tin, copper, and other alloys.

The metal boy had a voice like a hinge. He could turn his head and blink his eyes. No one would mistake him for a real boy, but he wore a green felt cap on his head like a real boy.

The metal boy was curious about everything—about the world, about himself, about the metalsmith. Unfortunately for him the metalsmith lacked the patience of a real parent. He already had an apprentice, whom he expected to remain quiet at all times, even when the hairs on his forearm got singed. The apprentice regarded the metal boy with distrust.

Banished from the studio, the metal boy would often wait at the crossroads. He would stand there for hours. Sometimes a bird would land on his shoulder and the metal boy would attempt a conversation, but his voice would startle the bird, who would fly away. The crossroads was an excellent place to practice what the metalsmith called "shutting up."

One day a traveler arrived. The metal boy first observed the man from a distance. It was unclear whether he was injured or approaching with caution, but the traveler walked more slowly than most people. When he got closer the metal boy could see he had short, red hair and ears like jug handles.

"Hello," the metal boy said.

The traveler stopped. If he was a bird he might've flown away.

"You can talk," he said. "I thought you were a scarecrow."

"I can talk," the metal boy agreed. "Why do you walk so slowly?"

"I hurt my leg."

"How did you hurt your leg?"

The traveler resumed his weary pace. He appeared to be malnourished—the metal boy reached this conclusion because of how loosely the man's clothes fit. The metal boy didn't require food, nor did he require clothes, neither for warmth nor propriety, but he enjoyed wearing them, like his green felt cap.

"Who made you?" the traveler asked.

"The metalsmith."

"Are there other metal boys?"

"Only me. Mostly he makes tools of war—sometimes a plow or a doorknob. How did you hurt your leg?"

"The little people did it," the traveler said. "Do you mind if I sit?"

The man lowered himself onto a tree stump the metal boy had dragged to the crossroads for this very purpose. It had been a long time since the last traveler had rested there. The metal boy angled his shoulders to provide a column of shade.

"Why did the little people hurt your leg?" he asked.

"You know about the little people?"

"Yes."

"Then you know they can't be trusted. They said they'd bring me food if I shared my magic, but then I was attacked. I barely escaped with my life."

"You know magic?" the metal boy asked.

"I can make wishes come true. Have you ever wondered who decides? Well, I do."

The traveler's stomach rumbled. Both he and the metal boy looked where the sound had originated. Sometimes the metal boy's body made noises, but mostly it was gears turning. Once he'd swallowed a tulip. Another time he'd swallowed a frog. The frog had hopped all around, from one extremity to another, until the metal boy had opened his torso to release it.

"I suppose you're wondering why I don't wish for food," the traveler said. "I can't make wishes for myself, only others—that's how the magic works. But I *am* hungry."

"The metalsmith has food."

"Would you bring me some?"

"Yes."

"This metalsmith," the traveler mused, "you said he makes tools of war? Do you mean weapons?"

"Yes, for the soldiers."

"Maybe don't say the food's for me. You can bring it here and I'll eat it, then we'll go see him together."

The metal boy nodded. It was a gesture he'd

learned from watching the apprentice. The other boy—the real boy—risked taking a beating whenever he spoke. Once the metalsmith had whipped him so relentlessly that the apprentice couldn't stand for two days. The metalsmith had claimed he was exaggerating. Now the metal boy looked at the traveler's leg.

"The little people attacked you? You saw them?"

"I'll tell you when you come back with my food."

The traveler shooed him away. He squinted as the metal boy departed, taking with him the column of shade.

It was a long walk from the crossroads to the metalsmith's studio—the metal boy wouldn't return before dusk. He was resolved to find food, feed the traveler, and ask the little people for guidance. Luckily the metal boy was well acquainted. Of all the living things he'd encountered, including birds and frogs, the little people had been the kindest to him, always listening to his questions and giving thoughtful answers. If the traveler was lying the little people would say so. If he required a beating the metal boy would provide it.

He pictured the traveler's big ears as he walked. He—the metal boy—had none. He could wish for ears shaped like tulips, he thought. Or he could ask the metalsmith. Or he could wish. The metal boy happily adjusted his cap.

The Giants

A farmer maintained a tidy grove of orange trees in a corner of his property. One day he realized that several trees were missing, their roots pulled straight from the ground. The only explanation was giants.

It wasn't uncommon for giants to steal fruit. The farmer thought of them like any other pest—a certain amount of loss was to be expected. The giants' hands were too large to peel the oranges, so they swallowed them whole. They would shake the trees at the grove's edge and eat whatever fell.

It would be harvest season soon. The farmer

could afford to lose individual fruits, he thought, but losing whole trees would damage his crop. Even if he planted new trees to replace the old ones it would be years before they matured.

The farmer stared at the holes in the ground.

He decided to make piles of fruit. That way, he hoped, his orange trees would be spared. It was true that other pests would be attracted to the piles, but the giants could eat them too. Did giants eat meat? The farmer didn't know. He didn't care. He'd never thought kindly of giants and now he was beginning to despise them.

"Why not use poison?" his son asked.

The boy was helping the farmer pile the fruit. It was tedious work. Loose oranges would roll from the top to the bottom and have to be retrieved.

"And what—poison the fruit? No," the farmer said, and that was the end of that conversation.

The next day, the giants had eaten the piles of oranges and had also taken more trees. The farmer was so distraught that he forgot about his morning chores. While his cows mooed and the chickens waited to be let outside, he paced and stared at the new holes in the ground.

It wasn't long before his son brought up the idea of poison.

"What if a person eats a poison orange?" the

farmer mused. "Then no one would buy any of our oranges—did you think of that? Or what if it works and the giants die? Do you want to dig giant graves? You can't just leave them to rot."

"But there's already holes in the ground from the trees."

"No," the farmer said. "Skunks—we'll get skunks."

That was his new solution to the problem. If the giants could only locate the grove by smell, because their eyesight was so poor, then skunks would mask the scent of citrus. It would also be a *bad* smell, which would maybe drive the giants away. Yes, the farmer and his son would have to trap the skunks first, but it was no more time-consuming than making piles of oranges. Never mind that piling oranges had been a wasted effort—something had to be done.

Unfortunately the skunks were a disaster. They were vicious creatures—they bit the farmer and his son, and sprayed their scent everywhere. A person was forced to breathe through his mouth, and even then it coated his tongue. The skunks liked the oranges too. They ate more than the other pests combined and bred at an astonishing rate, so that soon multiple generations of skunks were living in the orange grove. It was true that the giants stayed away, but one problem was hardly better than another.

Again the son proposed poison—again, again, again. Maybe there wasn't enough to kill every skunk, he said, but enough to make a pile. What if the giants developed a new taste? How long would it take for them to eat all the skunks, the ones that had been poisoned and the ones that hadn't? He described skunks running for safety like oranges rolling from a pile. Clearly the idea excited him.

The farmer only gave the appearance of listening. He knew his orderly life was ruined. He should've been more upset, he thought, about his son's scheme and the state of his farm, but he found that he no longer cared. Perhaps the world had always trended toward chaos, and he'd only been standing in the way.

The skunks hissed. His son leered. The farmer went to free the cows and the chickens.

The Woodpile

The woodpile kept the fire burning all winter long. It was also a home to spiders, mice, and the little people.

A boy and his grandfather lived inside the house. The grandfather was very old. On days when he was feeling well he would sit by the fire. On days when he was feeling unwell he would stay in bed under a pile of blankets. He rarely complained about the cold, but sometimes the boy could see his breath in the air. Then he knew to feed the fire.

There was only one rule they lived by—every log from the woodpile had to be replaced. This meant the boy had to chop wood, now that the grandfather was too frail. It also meant the bottom of the woodpile could never be disturbed.

"We must give in order to take," the grandfather said.

One morning the boy awoke to ice and snow. A storm had developed during the night. The woodpile was dry and there was plenty of food in the root cellar, so the boy wasn't concerned, but it was impossible to stray from the house. The snow drifts were getting deeper by the hour. The boy hoped the storm would pass. He resolved to chop more wood on the following day.

But the storm persisted.

"I have to wait," he said the next morning. "Once I can walk to the grove I'll cut down a sapling tree."

"Remember," his grandfather told him, "we must give in order to take."

"Yes, but I must go outside in order to chop wood."

The grandfather grunted, so the boy put another blanket over him.

First the spiders came inside the house.

Previously they'd occupied the top layer of the woodpile, but now they crawled under the door. The boy stepped on as many as he could, bringing his heels down again and again. Those that survived made new homes in the rafters. There was nothing to eat—no fat, lazy flies—but still they wove intricate webs.

Next the mice came inside the house. Previously they'd occupied the middle of the woodpile, but now they tunneled into the root cellar. The boy put out saucers of dandelion wine, but the mice made babies faster than he could kill them. The boy found their droppings everywhere. He could hear them squeaking in the night.

One thing troubled the boy more than the spiders and mice. He hadn't disturbed the bottom of the woodpile, but soon he'd have to—it was inevitable. He assumed that's where the little people lived. What would happen when *they* came inside? The spiders had already occupied the rafters. The mice had occupied the root cellar. All that was left, the boy thought, was the space in between. The idea kept him awake while outside the wind blew.

Finally they ran out of wood. The boy had a choice to make—he couldn't wait any longer.

He took a blanket from his grandfather's bed and threw it on the fire. At first he was concerned it might smother the embers, but then the flame caught. The wool produced a smell like wet dog. After that the boy added more. The house filled with smoke, so much that it couldn't go up the chimney, and the boy, choking, had to open the windows and door.

Through the cloud he could see his grandfather's naked body. Embarrassed, the boy turned away.

The Emerald

An old woman was nearing the end of her life. Her family had gathered to distribute her wealth.

The old woman called her maid to her bedside.

"Take this," the old woman said. She pressed an emerald into her maid's hands. "Swallow it."

The maid considered the jewel. It was smaller than her fist, but not by much.

"Madam," she said, "I can't swallow this—it's too big."

"They'll search you when you leave. If they find it they'll keep it for themselves."

Then the old woman died and the maid was left holding the jewel.

The emerald would make her rich, she knew. More importantly, it would make her independent. No one would be able to tell her what to do. With not a small amount of discomfort, she managed to swallow it.

The maid left the room to inform the family.

The first person she encountered was the old woman's daughter, who was waiting in the hallway.

"Madam is dead," the maid said. Her throat was sore from passing the emerald and her voice sounded hoarse with emotion.

"Finally!" the woman exclaimed.

She took a step toward the bedroom, but then stopped to appraise the maid.

"What did you take?" she asked. "Empty your pockets."

So the maid did as she'd been told, understanding that the woman would confiscate whatever she found. Of course there was nothing *to* find, because there was nothing in the maid's pockets. The emerald was secure in her belly. As she submitted to the woman's search, the maid felt a terrible pain in her side. She grimaced and said nothing, and the pain subsided.

Once the woman was satisfied she hurried to the bedroom. The maid continued on her way with her pockets turned out for anyone to see.

The second person she encountered was the old woman's son. He was taking the stairs two at a time, rushing like he knew what had occurred. The maid had never seen him move so fast, but he paused before passing her.

"Where are you coming from?" he asked.

"From madam's bedside. She's dead now."

"Did you take anything?"

"Nothing," the maid said. "Your sister checked my pockets."

The man squinted at her turned-out pockets. At the same time she felt another pain in her side, lower than before. The emerald seemed to be sinking. The maid pressed a palm against her gut.

"Take off your shoes," the man instructed.

The maid did as she'd been told. He inspected her shoes one at a time, wrinkling his nose at the smell, before handing them back. Meanwhile the maid tried not to groan. With each passing minute her discomfort grew worse.

"You can go," he informed her.

The maid hurried down the stairs. She didn't even stop to replace her shoes. Before she could exit the house she ran into the old woman's granddaughter, the man's only child, standing in the foyer under a chandelier. The girl stared at her turned-out pockets and the shoes she was carrying.

"What's wrong with you?" the girl asked.

The maid couldn't stand still, so she hopped from foot to foot.

"Madam died, but I didn't take anything," she said. "You aunt checked my pockets—your father checked my shoes. Please, let me go."

But the girl blocked her path.

"Open your mouth," she said.

So the maid opened her mouth. She stuck out her tongue while the girl plumbed inside her cheeks, probing one side and then the other. The maid tried not to gag.

"Hold still," the girl said.

She reached all the way into the maid's mouth, past her tongue, and down her throat. The maid could feel the girl's elbow pressing against her esophagus—and then she was tugging on something. The girl braced her knee against the maid's chest. A moment later she disgorged the jewel.

The emerald flew from her hand. No sooner had it landed than it grew claws, a shell, and beady eyes. The emerald turned into a crab. The girl promptly stepped forward and crushed it under her heel.

The Outhouse

A family installed indoor plumbing. For the first time in their lives they had a toilet.

Only the grandfather was unhappy about this development. While the rest of the family waited their turn in the hallway, he loudly complained to anyone who would listen.

"Where does it all go?" he asked.

"Away from here," his son said. "What do you care?"

"Because a problem that goes away by itself comes back by itself."

Jamie Yourdon

The grandfather insisted on using the outhouse. This irked his son, who'd hoped to have the latrine filled, but he knew better than to object. His father had become stubborn with old age—any argument would increase his resolve. Sooner or later, his son thought, he'd grow tired of going outside. The appeal of indoor plumbing would sway him.

The grandfather vowed not to be swayed.

One night he made a discovery. There was a new moon in the sky when he went outside, so the grandfather carried a candle. Upon opening the outhouse door he saw a figurine standing on the shelf. The grandfather gasped, but he soon realized it wasn't a little person—the figurine was a toy, carved from wood, that someone had left behind.

The grandfather brought the toy inside. He assumed it belonged to one of his grandchildren, but when he examined the figurine he saw that it resembled him. Someone had painted features, in addition to carving arms and legs, and it was not unreasonable to say it looked like the old man. This seemed like a good reason to keep it, he thought. Certainly if he'd discovered a painting of himself in the outhouse he would've claimed that too.

The grandfather became fond of the figurine. He carried it with him all the time. Although the artist had painted pants and a sweater, the old man was concerned that his miniature might feel cold, so he asked his daughter-in-law to knit clothes for it. The rest of the family had mixed feelings. The children were frustrated they weren't allowed to play with it. The grandfather's son thought his obsession was strange, but he was also glad the old man wasn't standing outside the bathroom anymore, waiting to ambush people.

Then the figurine disappeared.

It happened in the night. The grandfather liked to sleep with his miniature on his pillow beside him, facing the ceiling, and one morning it was gone. The old man became convinced that he'd been robbed. First he blamed his grandchildren, but they had no place to hide stolen property. After he'd searched their bedroom he accepted that they were innocent. Next he blamed his daughter-in-law, but his son put an end to his accusations.

"No one stole your stupid toy," he said. "You probably left it somewhere by accident. Did you go to the outhouse last night?"

The grandfather tried to remember. If he *had* visited the outhouse he would've brought the figurine with him, but he couldn't be sure, nor could he admit to his uncertainty. His son treated him like a baby. Every time he forgot something or had difficulty hearing, it was an excuse to mock him. No wonder the grandfather argued about everything.

"Yes," he said. "I remember now."

After that the old man stopped using the outhouse. He waited his turn for the bathroom, like everyone else, and stopped wandering at night. His son welcomed the change—finally he could fill the latrine. But the grandfather never flushed the toilet. He made the next person clean up his mess, no matter his reason for visiting the bathroom, and it was unclear whether he was doing it on purpose. His family showed him the handle. They showed him the water tank. It was so easy to understand that a child could do it, but the next time they looked it was always full.

The Suitors

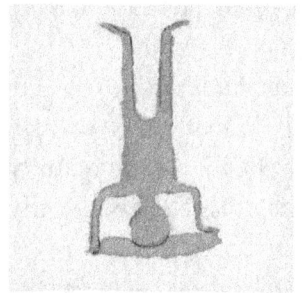

Two men were trying to impress a woman—they boasted and challenged each other to contests. The woman seemed to favor neither of them, but she enjoyed their attention nonetheless.

When a fourth person came along he was included in their affair. This other person had a secret. Whereas on the outside he might've looked like a normal boy, on the inside his bones were made of wicker. His arms and legs were as brittle as hay. The boy's father had been a scarecrow—his mother was a romantic.

The two suitors gave the wicker boy a glance and decided to ignore him. However, the woman spoke to him.

"Look at these two," she said. "Aren't they embarrassing?"

"I'm not embarrassed," the first suitor said. "He's the one who should be embarrassed. He can't even do a handstand."

"I can do a handstand if I want," the second suitor insisted. "I just don't do it all the time—unlike you. Maybe that's why your head is so big."

"My head is normal-sized."

"Normal for a melon."

The two men scowled at each other. Meanwhile the wicker boy said nothing. He was reluctant to get involved. To him, the suitors seemed unfriendly and the woman seemed irresponsible. Everything about the situation made him feel uncomfortable.

"What do you think?" the woman asked. "Should they stand on their heads?"

The suitors didn't wait for instruction. One balanced on his head for a short period of time before toppling over. The other balanced for longer, his neck and cheeks turned red from the effort. His head, the wicker boy observed, truly was large.

The woman yawned.

"That's not hard," she said. "What do *you* think—does it look hard?"

"It doesn't look easy," the wicker boy replied.

Still, the suitors glared at him. The one with the bigger head was slowly returning to his normal color.

"What should they do next?" the woman asked.

The wicker boy tried to think of something. He could tell the two men to race, in which case they'd both run away, but then he'd be alone with the woman. He could tell them to arm wrestle, but that was too much like fighting. The wicker boy didn't understand why he had to decide. No matter what he said there would be risk involved.

The woman was getting bored. She sighed and rolled her eyes. Finally the suitor with the smaller head spoke up.

"Tug-of-war!" he declared.

The woman clapped her hands in approval. The wicker boy was relieved not to have decided, but still eager to leave. While the two suitors were pulling on their rope and the woman was distracted, he could run away—that was his plan, anyway. He doubted anyone would follow him.

But there was no rope for the suitors to pull.

They looked around, as if a piece of rope might be lying on the ground. The wicker boy made a show of looking too. Maybe they'd lose interest, he thought.

"What about him?" the suitor with the bigger head proposed, meaning the wicker boy himself.

"Yes," the woman agreed, "use him."

The two suitors grabbed him. But the wicker boy wasn't a piece of rope—it wasn't obvious where he ended or where he began. Should they hold him by the ankles and wrists? Or should they each take an arm? No one asked the wicker boy what he thought. The woman just observed. She smiled like he deserved to be hurt.

The wicker boy could hear his bones fraying.

Sometimes wishes happened overnight. Sometimes they took days or weeks to come true, or even years. This time the wicker boy's wish was granted all at once and the woman disappeared. One moment she was watching them struggle and the next moment she was gone. There was no doubting she'd vanished, either. There'd been no time for her to run and hide.

"Oh, thank goodness," the first suitor said, releasing the wicker boy's legs. His feet landed with a thud.

"Yes," the second suitor agreed. "Thank goodness."

With greater care he lowered the wicker boy's arms, like he was spreading a picnic blanket over a patch of grass.

The Stationery

A pregnant woman had strong opinions about what she would eat. Sometimes she wanted nothing more than strawberries and potatoes. Other times the smell of chicken would make her gag. Her husband, who prepared all their meals, tried to stay current with her likes and dislikes, but they were constantly changing.

One day the woman awoke with a new appetite—she wanted to eat paper. She'd never eaten paper before. She didn't know what it would taste like, but she could imagine the texture between her teeth.

Her husband, not knowing better, had brought her a breakfast of blueberry pancakes.

"Ugh," she said. "I don't want this."

"No? More for me."

The woman's husband frequently ate the food she'd rejected. Her pregnancy was making him fat.

"It smells terrible," she complained. "Won't you take it away?"

"Of course, dear. Just make me a shopping list—I'll get what you want."

The woman considered the scrap of paper he'd given her. She waited until her husband had left the room, then crumpled the shopping list and stuffed it in her mouth.

It wasn't as good as she'd hoped, but it was only one piece.

The woman plotted where she could find more paper. Her first thought was her stepdaughter, the child from her husband's first marriage. The girl always had her nose in a book. In fact she often came home from the library with a stack of books so she wouldn't have to make multiple trips. The woman wondered how those pages might taste—salty from the touch of so many fingers. She climbed out of bed to fetch her robe.

"What are you reading?" she asked when she found the girl. Interrupted from her book, her stepdaughter looked up with suspicion.

"Why?"

"I'm curious."

Reluctantly she explained the plot of the novel. The woman focused on the quality of the paper—so thin it was nearly translucent. She imagined the pages melting on her tongue, the bitter ink staining her teeth.

"Can I borrow it?"

"I'm not done yet," the girl protested.

"What else have you got?"

The stepdaughter lowered her gaze to the woman's belly.

"You're acting weird," the girl said.

The woman was forced to reconsider. She didn't feel like leaving the house. What other paper could she find at home—wall art? Then she had an idea. For her wedding her mother-in-law had given her personalized stationery. The woman had used a few pages to write thank-you cards, primarily to her mother-in-law's friends, and had put the rest in the closet.

Now she found the stationery right where she remembered. Delighted, the woman carried it to her bed. She removed the lid and lifted the top sheet of paper. The page featured her name spelled in cursive, but, noticeably, not her husband's name. The woman's stomach rumbled. She raised the page to take a bite.

Abruptly her appetite changed.

She no longer wanted to eat the paper. It wasn't that she *didn't* want to eat paper, like she didn't want to eat chicken—a nauseating thought—but the idea no longer appealed to her. The page, still beautiful, bowed between her fingers. The woman felt a loss so severe that she nearly cried.

It was then that her husband came back.

"Oh good," he said. "You're making a list."

"No."

"No?"

The woman fought back tears, not wanting to explain. She placed the stationery on top of the pile and closed the lid.

"I don't want to make a list," she said. "I want you to remember what I say."

Her husband nodded, listening. He listened so intently that he seemed to vibrate.

The Chicken Coop

A soldier decided to leave the prince's army. Was he still a soldier after deserting his post? The army would've said yes, but the soldier would've said no.

The soldier planned to walk home, where he'd resume a normal life as something else. Perhaps he'd work in a hotel, as he'd done in his youth. He was traveling in the opposite direction from the army, hoping not to get caught, so mostly he traveled by night. During the days he would hide.

One morning the soldier hid in a chicken

coop. It wasn't the ideal place for him to rest. He would've preferred a cave in the woods, though those could be popular with bears. Haylofts got hot during the afternoons. The chicken coop would also be hot, and loud, and full of feathers, but the sun was already up.

"Hello," one of the chickens said as the soldier climbed inside.

The soldier didn't reply. The coop was snug, with a low ceiling. The air reeked of ammonia.

"Excuse me," the chicken said again. "This is a chicken coop, not a person coop."

"Don't worry," the soldier said. "I won't stay long."

He lay down on the floor and stretched out his legs. He considered making a pillow for himself, but thought otherwise when he looked at the feathers all around him, which were motley and stiff. Instead he folded his palms under his cheek. The soldier was very tired. He expected sleep to come easily.

However, the odor of chicken shit was too intense—it filled his nostrils like a barn on fire. The soldier tried to breathe through his mouth, but the smell became a flavor on his tongue and he gagged. Finally he pulled his collar over his head.

With his chin pressed against his chest all he could smell was his own sweat. It had been many days since he'd last bathed, but it was an improvement.

"What are you doing?" asked the same chicken as before.

"It stinks in here," the soldier said.

"It's a chicken coop, not a person coop."

Even under his shirt, the soldier discovered, it was too bright for him to sleep. Sunlight bounced off the painted wood and pierced the darkness. Frustrated, he poked out his head—choking on the smell—and tore a strip of fabric from his shirt. He tied the blindfold around his eyes. When he put his face back inside his shirt it was somewhat darker.

"Better?"

"Shut up," the soldier growled.

It was darker, yes, but now he was forced to listen to the chickens—really *listen*. He could hear their talons scratching the wood. He could hear them grunting as they laid their eggs. Most of all he could hear their inane conversation.

"Don't you ever shut up?" the soldier complained.

"I told you, it's—"

"Yes, yes, I know."

Soon he could hear another sound—a gentle

pawing coming from outside the coop. The chickens heard it too. Finally they were quiet, straining to listen.

"Who's there?" the soldier asked.

The pawing stopped.

"A wolf?" the soldier guessed. "Tell me, brother wolf, where you sleep is it very dark?"

"Yes," the wolf confirmed after a moment.

"And silent?"

"Yes."

"What does it smell like?"

"It smells like the earth."

"If I let you inside," the soldier asked, "and turn my back on whatever happens next, can I sleep there?"

The chickens were urgently opposed to this idea. They flapped their wings and flew from their roosts, but the soldier ignored them. He kept his chin tucked to his chest and listened for the wolf, who was weighing his decision. After all, a good den was hard to find.

"Yes," the wolf said. "I agree."

So the wolf gave the soldier directions and the soldier let him inside. They passed each other with a familiar nod. As promised, the wolf's den was silent and dark. The smell wasn't unpleasant. The

Jamie Yourdon

soldier lay with his arms folded against his sides and his nose buried in the soil.

The Poison Cup

News reached the prince of an assassination attempt. According to his spies, the would-be assassin meant to poison his cup.

The prince's mother, the queen, no longer lived at the palace. She'd moved to a private cottage shortly after the king had died. Now the prince went to visit her. He wasn't concerned for his mother's safety. Anyway, he'd assigned extra guards to protect her.

"They say he'll use a poison cup," the prince

said. "Can you imagine that—trying to poison *me*?"

"Attempts were made on your father's life too. One assassin even fed his beard into an apple press."

The royal marriage had been a matter of convenience, with the purpose of producing an heir, the prince. Because of their age difference it had come as no surprise when the queen had outlived the king. She still wore mourning colors, the prince observed, though, in his opinion, enough time had passed.

The queen was folding laundry, one black blouse after another. The prince wished she would stop and listen.

"Do you think the cup would be poisoned?" he asked. "Or the poison would be inside the cup? I think the first makes more sense—like, poison glaze. That way, it doesn't matter what I'm drinking."

"Do you know why they want to kill you?"

"Why?"

"If someone is willing to trade their life for yours," the queen said, "there must be a reason. Your father's siblings were always desperate to inherit the throne."

The prince thought about his uncles and aunt, who lived to the west, east, and south, respectively. All three had children, his cousins, though the prince didn't feel a kinship with them. He knew he could have them rounded up and thrown in the dungeon if he liked. The prince wasn't sentimental.

The queen was putting away her clothes, which she'd finished folding. Her chest of drawers looked rickety. The prince wondered if she'd acquired it secondhand. He tried not to look at his mother's undergarments.

"Do you know?" she asked again.

"No," he grumbled.

The queen came to him. She took his face in her hands.

"I'm sure you're doing a good job."

"Thanks, Mom," he muttered.

"I mean it—I'm proud of you."

"Like I don't have servants tasting my food," the prince said, grinning at the idea. "What idiots! Do they think I'll swallow anything?"

The queen sighed. She went back to putting away her socks, which she'd bunched in tiny balls.

"I hope you pay them well," she said, "the people who taste your food."

The prince didn't know what to say. It hadn't occurred to him that his servants were paid—that tasting his food might be somebody's job. As far as he was concerned everyone had a role to play. His role was being the prince. A servant's role was being a servant. Anyway, his mother seemed to be missing the point.

Outside, one of his generals was waiting to confer with him.

"Your Highness," the general said. "What should we do about the prisoner?"

The prince hadn't mentioned to the queen that his assassin had been caught—that his spies had volunteered a name as well as a method. He'd been too distracted by her questions.

"Kill him," the prince said. "I mean, obviously."

"Should we interrogate him first?"

"No, it doesn't matter what he says. Do we have an apple press?"

"Yes, Your Highness."

"Good, use that."

The Roots

A child was surprised to learn that plants grew down, into the dark, as well as up toward the light.

"Let me show you," her mother said.

Together they went to the garden. The mother pulled a weed from the ground, something the child had watched her do a hundred times before. But this time she noticed a bundle of roots. The pale threads clung to the dirt and only reluctantly came free.

"You see?" her mother said. "Above and below."

"Are all plants the same?" the child asked. She was looking at the tomato trellises, the zucchini flowers, and even the trees—plants all around her.

Her mother laughed.

"Of course they are! Right now, even as we speak, they're growing in both directions at once."

"What else grows down?" the child asked. "Not people?"

Something about the question irritated her mother, who made a sour face. But how could the child learn if nobody told her? Her parents had always marked her height against the wall. They'd commented on how tall she was getting. She'd never imagined that anything could grow in secret.

Sometimes her mother became impatient. Now she began to pull more weeds, indicating their conversation was over, and the child joined her, feeling guilty. She hadn't meant to test her mother's knowledge. The roots came free with a ripping sound.

That night it was difficult to sleep. The child wiggled her toes under her blanket. She thought of what she'd asked her mother—what else grew down as well as up? Not people. Not birds or animals, but other things? In the darkness the house made sounds. The floorboards creaked and the windows rattled, and the child realized, with alarm, that the house itself was growing down, even as she lay in her bed.

So she ran to the root cellar.

Here was a place she rarely visited. The child had brought a candle, and she carefully descended to the dirt floor. The root cellar was quiet—there was no more rattling or creaking from above. The child didn't know what to expect, so she looked left and right, moving her candle to shine a light. Something brushed against her shoulders.

She looked up.

Roots were draped from the ceiling. Some were thin and some were thick, and some were very thick. The child assumed they belonged to all different kinds of plants—weeds, trees, and everything in between. The roots filled the space above her head. Among the pale threads, she saw, there were also legs. Some of the legs were old and wrinkled, and some were quite young. The child didn't think she could recognize a person by her legs, but immediately she knew her mother, whose toenails were painted a garish red.

The child poked the arch of her mother's foot and watched as her whole leg twitched. Then she held the candle closer. She brought the wick under

Jamie Yourdon

her mother's toes, expecting to feel fear or shame, but she felt neither, not even as the foot curled. What feeling was it, then?

The Dancing Soldiers

The prince's army was camped outside a small town. The soldiers had been away from their homes for a long time.

In order to boost morale the officers organized a dance contest. The local auction house wasn't large enough to host such an event. The town square could accommodate more people, but there was concern it might rain. Finally everyone agreed on a barn. The soldiers' attitude was upbeat as they swept the floor and hung lanterns from the ceiling.

Every young man boasted that he would win the contest.

Jamie Yourdon

The rules were simple—two partners to a team, with a panel of judges to eliminate contestants. Because the soldiers outnumbered the townspeople three-to-one, there would be no restrictions on who could join, whether they be male or female, young or old, married or unwed. The only prohibition was that two soldiers couldn't dance together. Teams would be decided shortly before the contest began and prizes would be announced as the evening went on.

One woman was especially excited. She wasn't a dancer—the best she could do was sway back and forth—but she had aspirations beyond winning the contest. This woman had lived in the small town her entire life. She knew all the young men her age, as well as their older brothers. The idea of an entire army camping nearby had been thrilling to her and now she had an excuse to meet the soldiers.

When the teams were announced, shortly before the music started, the woman was paired with a soldier with red hair and big ears. It happened fast—an officer was reading names of enlisted men and pointing to the crowd of townspeople, barely leaving time for the teammates to acknowledge each other. The redheaded soldier looked to be roughly the same age as the woman and no taller than she. Her disappointment must've registered on her face, but he didn't flinch.

"I'm Felan," he said.

"Come on," she replied, turning and walking toward the dance floor.

The band was a mix of soldiers and locals. They played the same song over and over again, neither too fast nor too slow. At first the woman paid little attention to Felan. She absently registered his hand on her back as she glanced at her friends, some of whom had been paired with taller, more attractive soldiers and others who'd fared worse than she. There were fat soldiers and skinny soldiers. Dozens more stood by and observed. As she watched, a joking young man tried to dance with a barnyard cat, but the cat hissed and straightened its back, and the soldier threw it away.

"Enjoy it while it lasts," Felan said in her ear.

"What?"

"Trust me," he said, "it doesn't end well."

The judges began to disqualify contestants.

They walked among the dance partners, discreetly touching people on the shoulder. Many responded with a shrug. Some even looked relieved. But others muttered and scowled, and one team sneaked back on the dance floor and had to be disqualified twice.

The woman gradually realized that Felan was an experienced dancer. She followed his lead as he guided her around the barn, keeping their distance from the judges, who were more conspicuous now that the competition had thinned. She noticed other things about Felan too. He had good teeth. His posture was straight and his hands were dry, though her own were damp. She imagined him as an old man, and the idea made her smile.

"What so funny?" he asked.

"I think we could win," she said, ignoring his question. "There's not many people left."

Felan scoffed at her.

"They said there'd be prizes," the woman insisted.

"The only prize will be losing their tongues—*snit, snit, snit*."

Trouble started when the soldiers began to dance together. Some of the men thought it would be funny to grab a partner and twirl him around, but others did not. Soon a fight broke out. As the woman watched, soldiers punched or wrestled with each other. She didn't know what to do, but Felan kept dancing, even when the brawl spilled outside the barn. The music continued. It didn't sound as loud in the woman's ears, but always at the same pace, neither too fast nor too slow.

She could smell smoke. The same barnyard cat dashed by their feet. Someone or something had ignited the hay and now the whole structure was burning—flames climbing the walls and ceiling. People were coughing as they staggered outside. The woman tried to free herself from Felan's grip.

"Not until the song is over," he said. "Can't you hear it?"

Faintly, she could.

The woman's throat felt swollen. Her cheeks were taut. Felan held her close as she shuffled her feet.

The Grudge

A poacher was checking his traps when he discovered a grudge.

The poacher approached with caution, seeing the grudge was still very much alive. It had teeth everywhere, like a zipper that wound around and around its head. Its limbs appeared to be weak. It didn't run when the poacher set it free but cowered and nipped at him.

The grudge was a problem for the poacher. Clearly it belonged to someone else, but would its owner come looking for it? If the grudge was found to be injured—or, worse yet, if it died from its injuries—would the poacher be held responsible? The country bailiff had rules about how many traps a person could set. Occasionally the poacher bent those rules.

The best thing to do, he determined, was to restore the grudge to good health. Then it could then go home or somewhere else, where it would no longer be his problem. Avoiding the grudge's teeth, he bundled it in a sack.

The poacher reluctantly shared his cottage with the grudge. He would've preferred to keep it outside, but the nights were cold and the poacher worried about wolves and bears, so the grudge earned a place by the stove. At first it peed everywhere. The poacher's cat was understandably vexed. She spent hours hiding under the bed. The poacher never gave the grudge a name, but he did bathe it. He even brushed its teeth—a challenging and thankless task.

The grudge left when the weather changed.

It was the early days of spring. The poacher thought the grudge must be exploring beyond the cottage, but soon he realized it was gone for good. He checked his traps, knowing the grudge wouldn't make the same mistake twice. It was nowhere to be found. The grudge was gone.

The poacher felt sad. He hoped the grudge

would find its way home. He wondered if its owner would observe his diligence—how the grudge had been fed and cared for, with trimmed nails and healthy gums. The poacher even imagined seeing the grudge if he had business in town. Would the grudge recognize him? Would it run toward him and lick his face?

He didn't realize that his cat was pregnant. He attributed her strange behavior to being a cat—vomiting, sleeping, acting sluggish. It was only when she made a nest for her kittens that he understood her recent weight gain. The poacher assumed the grudge must've been the father. He didn't know how to feel. Surprised? Happy? Maybe it was foolish, but he was disappointed by his cat's secrecy.

When the time came for his cat to give birth she went missing, despite the poacher keeping a close watch. Her bed by the stove was empty. The poacher was certain she'd gone into labor because he could hear her moans—a terrible, unnatural sound that carried throughout the forest.

So he went to find her.

It was dusk—light still played among the higher branches of the trees, but it was dark on the ground. The cat's cries were directionless. The poacher was concerned that something else might find her, something with an appetite, so he ran, not knowing where to run. He flailed and thrashed through the understory.

That's when he heard the grudge. How did he know it was the grudge? Because no animal could make a sound like that. The poacher threw back his head and returned the call.

The Darning Bag

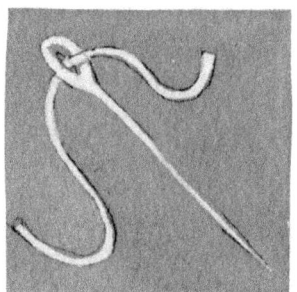

An old woman did all the mending for her family. Whenever a hole developed in someone's sleeve she would take out her darning bag.

"You're always putting things in your darning bag," the woman's granddaughter said. "But I never see you with a needle and thread. When do you fix our clothes?"

"After you've gone to sleep."

The old woman's granddaughter was an inquisitive child. She'd watch as her father split wood, as her mother kneaded dough, and as her brother picked his nose. She wasn't satisfied with her grandmother's answer.

So the girl worried a hole in her sock, which she gave to the old woman to mend. That night the girl stayed awake longer than her grandmother, watching as she fell asleep by the fire, and in the morning she was the first to rise. The girl had ensured this by drinking a large glass of water. By dawn her bladder was painfully full.

"Grandmother," she asked, "how did my sock get mended?"

"What do you mean? I mended it."

"When you put the sock in your darning bag it had a hole. When you took it out the hole was gone."

"You're mistaken," the old woman said. "Stop snooping."

The girl had a theory—she believed that little people lived inside the darning bag. Because she knew her grandmother wouldn't confess, and because she was determined to find out, the girl borrowed her father's ax and chopped off her thumb. Her plan had been to injure herself only a little, but the ax was heavy and cut through the bone.

"Grandmother!" the girl yelped. "I need your help!"

"Foolish child, what have you done?"

"Give me your darning bag—let me put my hand inside."

There was blood everywhere. In her haste the girl had lost track of her thumb, which had come off perfect and whole. She stuck her hand in the darning bag, but nothing happened. She didn't feel any repairs being made to her maimed finger.

The girl was bleeding quite a lot—so much that the bag was leaking.

"I think I'm going to faint," she moaned.

It was her nose-picking brother who saved her life. He applied their mother's dough as a compress—dough intended for meat pie, rolled thin and sprinkled with flour. The boy blotted his sister's wound and wrapped her hand until the bleeding had stopped. As she'd predicted, the girl had fainted. Her face was as white as their mother's flour, but slowly color returned to her cheeks.

No one had thought to retrieve her thumb. Only later did she ask about it, and by then her grandmother had baked the missing digit. Using some of the leftover dough, she'd made a special meat pie for the little people, who accepted her offer in good faith.

The Statue

One morning the residents of a village discovered a statue. Where there'd been nothing before, now it stood in the middle of their homes.

The statue was of a man. At first glance no one recognized him—his face wasn't especially handsome or noble. It wasn't meant to be the prince, that much was certain.

The statue was twice the size of a normal man. Many of his proportions were off, such as his arms being longer than his legs and his hands being larger than his head. The statue stood with a clenched fist.

Some villagers referred to him as the reaching man.

There were no signs of a horse and wagon, which would've been necessary to make such a delivery. No one had seen the statue being installed. The only potential witness was an old man who slept outside, but his account was unreliable. When questioned he first denied everything, including the statue itself. The old man was used to being made a scapegoat.

The statue was difficult to ignore. In addition to everything else, it took up a lot of space.

Since they hadn't requested it, and since they were uncertain who was responsible, the villagers decided to cover it up. A tarp was fetched from somebody's barn and thrown over the reaching man. A cheer went up from the crowd, like a victory had been achieved, and then the people dispersed. It was nearly their lunchtime.

Later in the day word got around that the statue had uncovered himself. People went to investigate and saw it was true—the reaching man was no longer covered by the tarp. He stood as before, only now the tarp was gripped in his fist, though, of course, that was impossible. The reaching man could no more grasp the tarp than he could pick his nose. Probably it had been disturbed by the wind, people said, and had become tangled.

But what if whoever was responsible for the statue was hiding in the village? Maybe the person had stayed to observe their reaction and had removed the tarp when they weren't looking. This scenario was also implausible, since the village was small, with few places to hide, but it angered the crowd. They felt they were being mocked. It was no longer sufficient to *mask* the statue—now they decided to bring it down.

A noose was tied and thrown around the statue's neck. All the men took turns pulling, including the younger men who still lived with their parents. At dinnertime, instead of sharing food, people drank wine. They spoke in loud voices about how ugly the reaching man was, how awkward his palms and limbs, as if their complaints could reach his ears. The statue groaned as they pulled. It was harder work than they'd expected.

When finally the reaching man came down, his collapse made a terrible sound. People cheered again, but with less enthusiasm than before, maybe because it was late and they were tired, or maybe because they were headachy from so much wine. The statue was left on the ground. Everyone went home, to bed, and no one seemed concerned that they were being watched.

In the morning the statue was gone.

Again there were no reliable witnesses. No one had seen or heard a thing. In fact no one had ventured outside until late the following morning, because they hadn't wanted to deal with the aftermath. Only the old man who slept outside claimed to know what had happened.

The statue had wept, the old man said. After everyone had gone away he'd bawled like an angry child. Then he'd departed, taking the noose from around his neck and throwing the tarp into a nearby tree, where it remained. He'd limped as he'd walked, the old man said, because the villagers had damaged his legs. He'd made threatening gestures at their houses. It was lucky he hadn't become violent. Just imagine the damage he could've caused, with his long arms and giant hands!

The way the old man spoke, he almost sounded excited.

The Heat Wave

A heat wave had gripped the countryside. Only the insects seemed content.

Families cowered inside their homes. They blocked their windows with patchwork quilts and lay upon the floor. Outside, the sun was like a vicious beast. Crops wilted in the fields, puddles evaporated without a sound, and even the crows refused to fly—walking instead, and muttering to themselves.

It was difficult to sleep at night. The touch of flesh to flesh was unbearable. People tossed and turned and perspired in their beds, while dreaming of winter, when their knees would ache from the cold.

A woman exited her home before dawn.

She'd left her husband and child still sleeping. It was the coolest part of day, when a faint breeze could bring some mild comfort. As she walked, the sweat dried on her neck and forehead. She would only go as far as the road, she'd decided, and turn back when the sun emerged.

Ahead of her she saw another person. He was a stranger—she could tell from a distance, with his back turned, though she wasn't alarmed. It was too hot to be riled.

"Hello," she greeted him.

The man had been stretching his arms—reaching for the sky with clenched fists. He turned to her and smiled.

"Hello," he said.

"May I join you?"

"Of course. I was just thinking about the little people—whether they suffer from the heat too."

"I don't see any tracks," the woman said.

"Me neither. Mostly I see spider webs."

The stranger's voice was like a song. He sounded amused by the things he was describing, or amused to share them with her, which made the woman feel shy. She wanted him to speak more.

"What's your name?" she asked.

The man squinted, but he didn't answer her question. Already the sun was bleaching the color from the sky.

"Ask me tomorrow," he said.

All day long the woman felt like she was keeping a secret—and she was, in a sense. She didn't tell her husband that she'd met the stranger or ask whether they had a new neighbor. She commented on the impressive size of the spider webs and her husband agreed, but it was all they could muster on the subject. Their child was too young to notice the heat. She pulled at the quilts hanging over the windows with surprising determination.

That night the woman couldn't sleep, and not for the usual reasons. The stranger had said "ask me tomorrow," implying they would see each other again. The woman was concerned about missing their appointment. What if she didn't wake up on time? What if her husband asked her where she was going or if her daughter needed her? So much could go wrong. The woman resolved that nothing would stop her. No matter what, she thought, she would reach the road by dawn—and, of course, nothing went awry. She slipped from her bed, opened the door, and stepped forth.

The stranger was waiting in the same place. The woman's heart fluttered in her chest.

"Good morning," she said.

"Good morning. Did you see any little people?"

"No, but I've been thinking—maybe they've all gone away. Maybe the heat is *because* they've left. They were keeping us safe the whole time."

"It's possible," the man agreed. "My grandmother said that little people were here before us and then we came along. I suppose there's always someone bigger and someone smaller."

The woman thought of her daughter tugging at the quilts. The day before they'd taken turns placing their ears against the floor while the other had stomped her feet. Was that how they sounded to the little people? Like the whole earth was shaking?

"Did she raise you?" the woman asked. "Your grandmother?"

She wanted to know more about the stranger— where he was from, what his childhood had been like—but already the man was squinting. The woman glanced at the horizon. The needed more time, she thought. They'd only had a few minutes together.

"Ask me tomorrow," the man said.

The following day was unbearable. The woman couldn't stand to be around her family. Her daughter was needy and her husband was idiotic. It was torturous to be trapped inside with them and even worse to be outside, where the air was like a furnace. The woman retreated inside her mind. She recalled the slope of the stranger's neck and the breadth of his shoulders. She tried to guess his name, knowing that all her guesses would be wrong. Somewhere he was also passing the time. Was the stranger thinking about her? Was he agitated too?

The next morning the heat wave broke—the woman could feel it when she stepped outside. The air was cooler, almost cold, and she hugged herself for warmth. Then she ran. It didn't matter that she was barefoot and the ground was littered with sharp stones. She was certain, even before she arrived, that the stranger would be gone, but she had to know for herself.

The Pillow

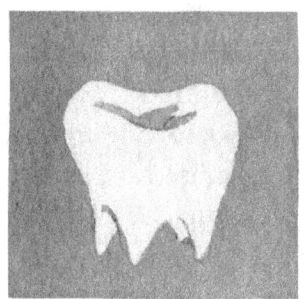

A man was raising his daughter by himself. His wife, the girl's mother, had died from a mysterious illness the year before. After days of fevers and hallucinations, she'd been gone.

The girl had no friends, but she was self-sufficient, for which the man was grateful. She never clung to his leg. She prepared their meals but otherwise spent her days outside the home. Soon she'd be old enough to do laundry. Then she could earn money by cleaning the neighbors' clothes.

One night, as the man was putting his daughter to bed, he discovered something under her pillow.

"What's this?" he asked, withdrawing his hand.

There were dozens of flower petals beneath the girl's head—pink, delicate, and fragrant.

"Where are they from?" the man asked.

There were no flowering trees on their property, meaning the girl had found the petals elsewhere. The man was reminded of how much time his daughter spent alone and how little he knew about her days.

The girl didn't reply. She stared at her father with the covers drawn up to her chin. It wasn't bad or wrong for her to collect flower petals, he thought. He kissed her on the forehead, as was their custom.

But the next evening, when he put her to bed, he discovered something new beneath his daughter's pillow.

"Are these feathers?"

The man needn't have asked. The feathers were white—likely belonging to a dove, he thought. The man and his daughter didn't keep doves. There was blood on the quills, suggesting they'd been forcibly removed.

"Where did you get these?" he asked.

His daughter stared at him with wide eyes. Had she collected the feathers from a neighbor's aviary? Or had she plucked them from unwilling birds? The man didn't know, but he hadn't told her not to gather flower petals. Did that make it his fault?

"No more," he said. "Do you understand me? No more feathers, no more flowers."

But the following evening he made a worse discovery.

Teeth.

There were human teeth under her pillow, as many as twenty. The man's first thought was to check inside his daughter's mouth, but he knew they didn't belong to her. Where had they come from? Not from living people, he hoped, but not from dead people, either. There was no answer that would soothe him.

"What have you done?" he shouted in distress.

The man stood up and stumbled, dropping the teeth in his haste. The girl looked from her father to the floor, where the pale enamel flashed in the darkness.

"I'll go find the country bailiff and beg forgiveness," he said. "I beg you—do nothing. For the love of your mother, who would've known better what to do, do *nothing*."

After the man was gone, a barnyard cat came through the window, followed by another cat, and then another, until there were so many cats in the girl's room that they occupied every surface—cats cleaning their paws, cats flicking their tails. Outside she could hear even more.

"You have to stop," the girl insisted. "No more presents."

"You don't like them?" one of the cats replied.

"My father is upset. He's gone to see the bailiff."

A gray cat jumped onto the girl's bed. It paced the length of her legs and settled in her lap, where it licked her wrist with its sandpaper tongue.

"Come away," the cat encouraged her.

"I don't know yet. I haven't decided."

"Yes, you have."

The Shears

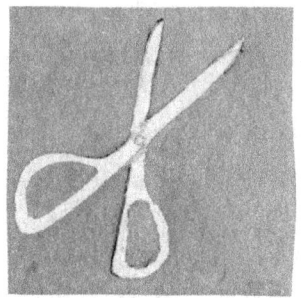

A seamstress had a special pair of shears that she used only for tailoring, lest their blades get dull.

Every year, in the spring, a cutler would visit her village. Using a combination of stones and sand he would sharpen knives, scythes, and even ice skates, asking for trade in return. The seamstress mended his winter garments. The cutler traveled in all different weather and depended on the seamstress to keep him warm and dry.

One year he didn't come. No one ever knew the reason why.

The seamstress's shears remained sharp, but only because she used them sparingly. They continued to make a satisfying noise whenever she cut fabric—a *snit* as the two blades nested together. A person could imagine how well they'd work in the hands of anyone else, whether the florist or the butcher. After all, the seamstress's shears didn't know what they were cutting, only *snit, snit, snit*.

Meanwhile the other blades in the village became increasingly dull. People sawed at tomatoes with their knives. They hammered at logs with their axes. The cutler's absence was felt by one and all.

The day came when someone asked to borrow the seamstress's shears. It was the chandler, her neighbor and friend. His own shears had become too dull to cut the wicks of his candles, probably because he used them in his garden. The seamstress watched him every evening. She'd seen how green and tacky the blades had become.

"Have you tried using your teeth?" she asked.

The seamstress demonstrated for him, using her own teeth to cut a piece of thread. She'd meant that the chandler could bite his wicks, though he also could've bitten the stems in his garden, she supposed.

The chandler looked disappointed, but acknowledged that he could do the same.

Next the midwife asked to borrow the seamstress's shears. She needed something to sever the cord between mother and child. The seamstress had never been fond of the midwife and assumed that the feeling was mutual. As someone without children, who had no desire for children, the seamstress had always suspected the midwife of condescending to her.

"Have you tried using your teeth?" the seamstress asked.

In the time of their mother's mothers women had routinely chewed the cord. Of course the midwife knew this. Like the chandler, she did a poor job hiding her disappointment, even looking a bit queasy, but she left without objection.

Finally the seamstress was visited by her friend the shepherd. His sheep had become heavy with wool since he'd stopped trimming their coats. It was dangerous for them, he said—in the coming months they could overheat and die. They already appeared sluggish, trudging from pasture to pasture, with the summer sun bearing down on them.

Here was a different situation—the seamstress couldn't tell the shepherd to use his teeth. At the same time, her shears wouldn't be enough. Even if she agreed, he couldn't trim his entire flock. He needed his own tools, with longer blades, for which he required the cutler.

The seamstress felt sorry for the shepherd and his sheep. His concern for his flock was genuine. She decided to help him, even if her shears weren't the solution he needed.

If the sun was the cause of the shepherd's problems, the seamstress thought, then he could tend to his flock at night. It would take some getting used to. The shepherd and his sheep would sleep during the day and roam the pastures in the evening, when the air was cooler and the sheep's coats weren't so uncomfortable. There was reason to fear the little people, but the seamstress, in her generosity, made a gift of her shears, and thereafter the little people granted the shepherd safe passage.

While the sun was out and the flock slept, villagers quietly walked by the sheepfold. While the moon and stars were out and people were asleep in their beds, the sheep were free to graze, their bells ringing in the night. And the little people made good use of their new shears, going *snit, snit, snit* as they cut out the tongues of the prince's army, leaving many of his soldiers maimed and mute.

The Locked Room

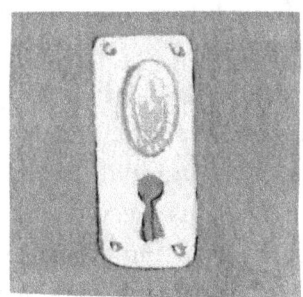

A sister and brother discovered a locked room in their parents' house. No other door was barred to them, not even the root cellar door with its steep steps.

"What's in there?" the boy asked.

The girl didn't know, but she was reluctant to admit it. She was the elder of the two and thus expected to have answers. With her ear against the door she could only hear the beating of her heart. She tried looking through the keyhole but could see nothing.

"It's a secret," she said, "and secrets are like poison. They can make you sick and die. We need a key."

So the children searched for a key.

The girl looked inside every pocket she could find, from the coats hanging by the door to the trousers in the closet. Any money she discovered, she kept for herself. Meanwhile her brother recalled a bowl of keys he'd seen in the root cellar. He carefully climbed down the stairs, braving the dark.

None of the keys worked.

"Maybe there's a window," the boy said.

A window to see inside! It was an excellent idea, though his sister neglected to say so since it hadn't occurred to her first. Instead she ran to the yard, around the side of the house, faster than her brother could follow. Being older also meant being taller, with longer legs.

Unfortunately there wasn't a window. This made the idea less excellent, which made the girl feel more charitable. Outside it had turned into a fine day. They could've abandoned their search and gone to play—on the climbing tree by the mailbox or down by the creek bed. They could've left the locked door for another time.

"Is it true that secrets make you sick and die?"

the boy asked when he'd caught up, breathing hard.

"Yes," the girl said. "Your eyes bleed. Your fingernails fall out."

"I don't want that."

"Then we need to open that door."

They went back inside, leaving the sunny day behind. The girl tried twisting the knob.

"Sister," the boy said. "I have a secret."

Once, when the girl had been sick and the boy had been sent outside to play, he'd made a new friend—a metal boy. This mechanical child had been crafted from tin, copper, and other alloys. His father had been a metalsmith, but that had been a long time ago. He was actually quite old, the metal boy had said. He'd traveled to many places and had seen many things, and now he was ready to die.

The metal boy had told his new friend not to be afraid. Just because he was dead didn't mean he would cease to be. A stone knew when it was being warmed by the sun. A divining rod could feel minerals in the dirt. The metal boy had enjoyed his life, but he believed there was more to experience. He only needed to find it.

Together they'd identified a heavy stone. The mechanical child had lain on his side, exposing one of his ears, which had been shaped like a tulip. Then the boy had raised the stone in both hands and had smashed the metal boy's head. He'd flattened his skull, which wasn't really a skull, and had left him there to rust.

"I never told anyone," the boy confessed, clinging to his sister. "I don't want my eyes to bleed."

The girl was speechless. She recalled having a fever. She remembered how her muscles had ached and her sheets had been tangled, and how she hadn't spared a thought for her brother. The fever had been like a bad dream, the worst kind of sleep. Yes, she'd imagined a metal boy, with ears like flowers, but where had the vision come from? How had she explained it to herself? The metal boy had been looking for something. He'd looked under her bed and even inside her mouth, forcing her to stick out her tongue. His fingers had tasted like dirt.

"Show me," she said.

The Portrait

A rich man hired an artist to paint his portrait. The artist was highly renowned. Everyone admired his work and his confident demeanor.

The rich man understood his portrait to be an investment. No matter how much he paid for it, the painting would become more valuable over time. In addition to acquiring an asset, he was also motivated to see the artist's likeness of him.

He was fascinated by the idea of being turned into art.

The two met every day at the artist's studio, where the rich man would pose for hours at a time. He found it difficult to sit still, but called upon his discipline, which had contributed to his fortune. He didn't flinch when a fly buzzed around his face. He didn't stand when his legs cramped. The artist praised him for his patience, saying he'd never had a better model, but he refused to show the rich man the unfinished portrait. Every time the rich man asked to see and the artist declined, their relationship became a little more tense.

"Don't forget that I'm paying you," the rich man said.

"How can I forget," the artist replied, "when you keep reminding me?"

One day the rich man failed to come to the studio. The artist waited for an hour then brought his sketchbook to a nearby café, where he ordered a glass of wine. He made three drawings—one of which he liked—and flirted with the waitress, who had a gap between her front teeth.

The next day the rich man's butler delivered a letter. He claimed it was from the rich man—the artist hadn't seen his handwriting before, but the voice sounded like him. In the letter the rich man explained he'd be gone for an indefinite period of time. He told the artist to keep the portrait and to accept full payment for his work. He apologized for the inconvenience.

The artist should've been happy, he thought—after all, he'd received his money. Who cared if the job went unfinished? He visited the café, where he ordered another glass of wine and flirted some more with the waitress, who smiled with her mouth closed, but his thoughts lingered on the unfinished portrait.

No one had ever fired the artist before. He didn't know what to do.

The artist went to the rich man's house, where he questioned the butler. No, the rich man wasn't home. Yes, he often traveled, but he hadn't said where he'd be going, or for how long, or why. No, there was no way for the artist to contact him. His disappearance would have to remain a mystery. The butler politely ended their conversation.

In the weeks to follow the artist found it impossible to work on anything else. Whether he tried to sketch or to paint, the portrait always occupied his mind. Sometimes he'd make a minor change, working around the edges of the rich man's likeness, but mostly he left it untouched. He couldn't go forward and he couldn't go back. He visited the rich man's house a second time, but the butler had no new information to share with him.

Then, one day, the rich man returned. The artist was informed by the waitress, who always knew the latest gossip. She said the rich man had been thrown from a carriage at night—a witness had been present—and was recovering from various injuries. No one could say who'd been driving the carriage or where the rich man had been, but people assumed the worst. The café had been especially busy, the waitress said. She'd made twice her normal amount on tips.

The artist had conflicting emotions.

Ultimately he decided to write a letter, not knowing what he meant to say. He didn't mention the rich man's absence. He didn't refer to the gossip, the rich man's injuries, or even bring up the portrait. With all those things excluded it was a very short letter. He invited the rich man to visit his studio. He said he looked forward to working together again. Despite being brief, it was the truth.

A day passed, during which time the artist felt irritable and distracted, and then, on the second afternoon, the rich man came to the studio. He arrived unescorted—he'd left his butler at home. The artist was stunned by the change to his appearance. The rich man's face was gaunt. He had bruises along his jaw, possibly from being thrown from the carriage, or possibly from being beaten. Most prominently, he was missing his left ear. The wound had been bandaged, but, from the flatness of the gauze, it was clear the appendage was gone.

    The two men sat and stared at the unfinished portrait. There was no discussion about what had occurred or how they might proceed. After a little while the rich man began to cry. He cried very gently, making sniffling sounds, until the artist got up and fetched him a handkerchief.

The Hanged Man

The army had disbanded and not by order of the prince. Some soldiers had remained loyal, but most had walked away, either returning to their homes or joining new communities.

It was the country bailiff's job to punish deserters. Of course it was difficult to prove that someone had been a soldier when the same person denied it, so he found them guilty of other things, like stealing. Then he'd see them hanged. The bailiff would shave their heads, as a reminder of their oath to the prince, and the traitors would be revealed.

A gallows had been erected in a small town. The bailiff stood in the shadow of the stage. He was fanning himself with his too-tall hat and interviewing a deserter, who sat on the lowest step, his hands tied behind his back.

"Do you have a name?" the bailiff asked. "Any family? Children?"

The deserter ignored his questions.

The bailiff only meant to notify next of kin, not to condemn anyone else, but it wasn't important. The deserter had no belongings, only the boots on his feet.

"It won't be long," the bailiff said.

"Take your time," the deserter replied. "I'm not going anywhere."

A small crowd had gathered—a carpenter and a mother with her three children. They seemed to be more interested in the gallows, which was taller than the fountain in the town square. The fountain itself was dry. The bailiff was only waiting for the hangman to return from lunch. He looked at the faces of the townspeople, but the mother and carpenter pointedly looked away.

The hangman was also local, but not the bailiff.

He'd been born two towns over, where his father still lived. The bailiff's father was old, too old to live by himself, yet somehow he managed. Lately he claimed to have befriended the little people. He left his doors and windows wide open, even in stormy weather, and responded angrily when anyone closed them. The bailiff shuddered to think what else might be living in his father's house—mice and spiders, most likely. What if a hungry bear came along? Would his father befriend him too?

The hangman came back with mustard on his shirt.

"This man is guilty of theft," the bailiff announced to the crowd, nodding at the deserter. "When neighbors steal from neighbors, communities suffer. The prince protects you. He promises swift judgment."

The mother applauded. From the stage the bailiff could see the carpenter admiring his work. It was true the gallows had been well constructed, and on short notice, but the real test would be the trap door—how quickly it responded to the hangman's touch.

"Do you have any final words?"

The deserter cleared his throat. The hangman

had shaved his red hair the night before, making his ears appear even larger—like jug handles, the country bailiff thought.

"Nothing matters."

"Excuse me?"

"Nothing matters and everything ends."

"Shame on you," the bailiff scolded him. "There are children present."

"Children," the deserter said, the noose cinched tight around his neck, "someday you will die. Your mother will die, all your friends will die, and everyone you know will be dead. It'll be like you never existed—like before you were born."

The bailiff felt faint. One town over his father was talking to the little people. He was climbing onto his roof to see giants. The fountain in the town square was dry.

"The lever," he barked at the hangman. "Pull the lever!"

The trap door opened. The deserter fell through the floor—the rope taut—and his neck audibly snapped, but the trap door was silent. The carpenter had oiled the hinge.

The eldest child ran under the stage. The bailiff couldn't see what he was doing—he could only see the child's mother, who stood with her arms around her other children, pressing their faces against her hips. He had a better view when he looked through the trap door. The eldest child was stealing the deserter's boots. He tugged on one, clearly expecting resistance, and tripped when it came off. The laces were still tied. Knotted and bowed, the bailiff mused, like a birthday present.

The Glut

A milliner had invested too heavily in the previous year's fashion. When tastes changed he was left with hundreds of hats.

He decided to sell his inventory through the auction house. By offering everything at a discount he hoped to recoup his loss. The milliner had debts to pay. Unfortunately no one wanted to buy one or two unfashionable hats—but possibly they would buy a hundred or more.

"How shall I advertise the lot?" the auctioneer asked.

"A glut of hats," the milliner replied, but then he corrected himself. "Just say a glut—a *glut* for sale to the highest bidder."

The advertisement inspired curiosity. A glut of what? Hats were the furthest thing from everyone's mind. For a week it was all the town could talk about—what the highest bidder might win.

"I bet it's a glut of envelopes," the grocer said, raising the subject with one of his customers.

"Why do you say that?"

"They stack easily, they never go bad, and everyone needs them—only, people buy them one at a time."

The customer nodded, appreciating his logic.

"I bet it's pigs," she guessed. "Albino pigs."

The milliner overheard many such conversations—at the café, even in his own store. He couldn't remember the last time the auction house had received so much interest. He was confident he would sell his lot and be free of his inventory. More importantly he'd have money to pay what he owed. But why do that, he thought, after being rewarded for his business savvy? He could double or triple his profit with some more shrewd decisions. His debtors could wait, the milliner told himself.

So he bought more fabric.

Jamie Yourdon

On the night of the auction it seemed like every man and woman was in attendance. The auction house was standing room only—every seat had been taken. The milliner had come to watch the bidding in person. The effort of keeping his role a secret, even from a few trustworthy associates, had been considerable, but he understood that the wrong word in the wrong ear could have a terrible effect.

The auctioneer started the night with some lesser lots—an oil painting, a half acre of land. Some people made bids, but mostly they shifted in their seats.

"Now we come to an interesting item," the auctioneer said. "A glut. What do I hear for this lot?"

A murmur went up from the crowd. People leaned forward with anticipation, waiting for someone to speak. The milliner held his breath.

"What is the first and lowest bid for this lot?" the auctioneer asked again.

As the wait grew longer, the milliner started to panic. Would nobody bid? Maybe he should? But what if he began the bidding too high or too low—would that impact people's decisions? Clearly they were intrigued or else they wouldn't be there.

"Will anyone start the bidding?" the auctioneer inquired.

"Show us what it is!"

It was unclear who'd spoken. The milliner thought it might've been the grocer, but no matter—the crowd cheered. Everyone wanted to see the glut. Maybe it was all they wanted, in which case they'd go home satisfied, or maybe they'd start bidding. Something good had to happen, the milliner thought. The alternative was ruin.

He caught the auctioneer's eye and nodded his approval.

"Very well," the auctioneer said. "Let's have a look."

The glut was concealed under a tarp. As the crowd voiced its encouragement, the auctioneer took ahold of one corner and pulled. All at once their celebration stopped—the crowd was stunned into silence. The glut wasn't an albino pig, that much was certain, but it *was* pale. It had a rank, animal smell. How had they not been aware of the smell? And how had it remained silent and motionless under the tarp? Now the glut considered their astonished faces.

Nobody moved until someone nudged back his seat, and then violence ensued.

The Grapes

A girl and her mother were starving. The girl's father had died the previous spring and the girl's mother was still grieving his loss. Now it was winter and there was nothing to eat.

So the girl went to visit the prince. He wouldn't want them to suffer—the prince's father had also died, the girl knew. The whole kingdom had mourned the loss of the late king. The prince would be doubly sympathetic when she explained their situation, or so she believed.

The prince was easy to find. He lived in a castle.

Any one of the prince's guards might've turned the girl away, but she was so plainspoken and resolute that they let her pass. Why wouldn't the prince want to help her? He might've helped more people if they'd asked him directly. Finally the girl stood before her monarch, who was seated on his throne, and made her case—how her father had died, how her mother was depressed, how they were hungry all the time.

"We need your help," she said.

"What's your favorite food?" the prince asked.

It wasn't the question the girl was expecting. She'd been prepared to explain the details of her father's death, which she would've preferred not to think about. Naming her favorite food required no thought at all.

"Grapes," she said.

So the prince sent grapes.

They started to arrive even before the girl had returned home—little, red grapes, tart, but not unpleasantly so. The girl and her mother were saved. They ate grapes by the bunches. They made grape ice cream and grape pie, and dried hundreds more for raisins. The girl's mother remained depressed, but at least she was eating, and the girl had the satisfaction of being right. She'd guessed the prince would help and indeed he had.

However, they soon tired of grapes. The girl's fingertips had been stained red. Whether or not they had been her favorite food, too much of a good thing was still too much. The girl thought about the prince's question and decided that, while it probably hadn't been a trick, she should've given a more nuanced answer. The prince wasn't known for being a creative thinker.

The second time she visited the castle the guards let her straight through.

"We need more variety," she told the prince.

The girl was mindful of her tone. She wanted to sound firm without also sounding ungrateful. She'd brought raisins to eat on her journey and now she played with them in her pockets—rubbing them between her fingers like balls of snot.

"What do you think happens when we die?" the prince asked.

"Excuse me?"

"When we die—I think we become birds. Have you ever wondered why there are so many? And why they sing? Dogs don't sing, they howl."

The girl was at a loss for words. She glanced at the guards, who avoided eye contact.

"I think my dad came back as a sparrow," he continued. "I don't know why he won't visit me—maybe because he doesn't remember me. Or maybe there are rules. It's not worth getting your feelings hurt, I say."

The girl's audience with the prince soon ended. Later she'd regret that she hadn't spoken up, offering her own insights about death. Who else would be willing to listen? The girl hadn't realized how lonely she felt. When she had been starving no one had looked at her and seen that she was hungry. Now it was the same, except no one knew how she was feeling.

The prince had been more attentive than she'd given him credit for. The grapes continued to arrive, as before, but with greater variety—green grapes, seedless grapes, grapes that tasted like spun sugar. The same person made the delivery, week after week, and soon the girl realized he was courting her mother, who bashfully returned his attention. The girl didn't know whether her mother was less sad because of her flirtation or the flirtation persisted because she was less sad. Either way it was nice to see. Her mother blushed every time he fed her a grape. It should've been embarrassing, but it wasn't.

Meanwhile the girl looked for her father in every bird she saw. Some welcomed her attention, but most flew away. The prince had been right—it wasn't worth feeling spurned.

The Siren

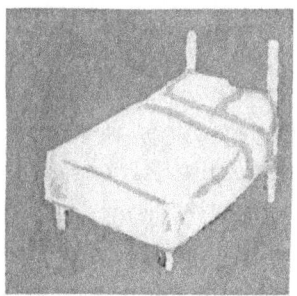

Once there was a family—a father, mother, and three daughters. The father worked all night as a watchman and the mother worked all day as a waitress.

The father would come home every morning as the girls were waking up. He was always tired, but he gave them each a kiss and listened as they described their dreams. Then he'd go lie down.

"Play quietly and let your father rest," the mother would instruct the girls. Then she, too, would give them each a kiss before leaving for work.

That was the only rule—not to wake their father. The girls could play games or make snacks, or even leave the house on a sunny day, but they must remain quiet until he awoke.

One morning the oldest daughter was making a marmalade sandwich. She dropped her knife, which fell with a clatter. The girls held their breath, wondering whether the sound would wake their father, but a minute passed and still he didn't emerge from their parents' bedroom.

The oldest daughter had an idea.

Grinning at her sisters, she opened the cupboard with the loudest hinge. Open and closed, open and closed—the hinge squealed as the girls muffled their giggles. No one emerged from their parents' bedroom. Again, their father had slept through the din.

The middle daughter was next. She ran outside while her sisters waited to hear what noise she'd make. Would she bring an animal inside the house? Maybe she'd find a chicken or a barnyard cat. Her older and younger sisters snickered. Then, from above, they could hear her—she was standing on the roof!

The middle daughter had climbed the trellis. Now she ran from one side of the house to the other, fast but not too fast, lest she fall. Her sisters followed her progress. They watched as dust rained down, agitating the spiders that lived in the rafters. Back and forth she went, and no one emerged from their parents' bedroom. Their father had slept through the din.

When she came down from the roof it was the youngest daughter's turn.

The youngest daughter had never won any of their games—or if she'd won it was because her sisters had let her. The youngest daughter knew this and didn't like it. She wanted to win because she was the best, not because of their generosity, but she didn't understand the contest. Was the point to make the loudest noise and *not* wake their father? Or was the point to wake him? She worried they might change the rules if she asked, so she kept her questions to herself.

The girl opened her mouth and made the loudest cry anyone had ever heard. AAAAAAAAAAAAAAAAAAAH. It wasn't a yell or a scream, more like a siren. They didn't know if she was in pain. She barely paused to breathe. The girl had become an instrument for sound.

Their father emerged from the bedroom.

"What's happening?" he asked, bleary-eyed. "What is it?"

He rushed to his youngest daughter and knelt

before her. Brushing the hair from her face, he stared into her eyes. He tried to comfort her, but she gave no reply—if she could even hear him—so he picked up his youngest child and ran for the door. The other girls followed him.

The father ran with her in his arms, pressed against his chest, still wailing. When he reached the town well, he stopped. Holding his youngest daughter under one arm he frantically tugged on the rope, pulling and pulling, until the bucket appeared, sloshing water. With his free hand he emptied the bucket over her head. The child spluttered and blinked her eyes. All at once the sound stopped.

The father slumped to the ground. His other daughters joined him there, all four of them panting.

"Papa doesn't have any shoes," the youngest girl observed.

It was true—he'd acted so fast, he was still barefoot. The girls looked at his feet and his rumpled pajamas and began to laugh. The father smiled. He wiggled his toes. Spreading his arms around his daughters, he pulled them close.

The Garden

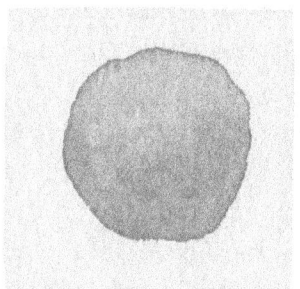

A child was left in his grandmother's care. Her home was unfamiliar to him, even though there were pictures of him on the walls.

"What should we do while Mommy and Daddy are away?" his grandmother asked, meaning the boy's mother and father. "We could work in the garden. Wouldn't that be nice?"

The boy wasn't keen to garden, but he'd rather be outside than inside, where he felt compelled to breathe through his mouth. Every room smelled the same in his grandmother's house, he thought. It smelled like her skin. The boy wondered if she even noticed.

His grandmother put on different clothes for gardening—gloves, a blouse, and a floppy hat. She gave the boy boots that were too big for his feet. Since she didn't have another pair of gloves, she said to dig for stones, which he could feel with his bare hands.

"Rocks and stones make it hard for roots to grow," his grandmother said. "That's not nice, is it?"

"No," the boy muttered.

He did as he'd been told while his grandmother occupied another part of the garden. He dug for rocks and stones, not knowing what made "rocks" different from "stones." He found it funny that so many were buried in the ground. He tried to imagine what a person could do with all that gravel—build a little wall, he supposed. A little wall for little people. That was funny too.

The boy threw a rock over his grandmother's house—he didn't see where it landed. He threw a second rock, this one larger than the first, and it struck the roof, making a satisfying sound. He threw a third rock and a fourth, no longer trying to clear the roof, and each of these rocks rolled down the other side.

As he cocked his arm a fifth time, his grandmother snatched him by the elbow. Her grip was surprisingly painful as she loomed over the boy.

"What are you doing?" she demanded.

"Nothing," he said.

"It's not nice to scare a person."

She let him go. The boy lowered his arm, rubbing the tender place where she'd squeezed him. For the first time he wondered when his parents would return.

A new task was assigned—pulling weeds. Most of the plants had sharp leaves, and without gloves the boy's hands were exposed. He tried to pull close to the root, but still they cut his palms. The boy knew he was being punished, and that his punishment would last as long as his grandmother was mad, but he was also mad. He didn't feel he'd done anything wrong.

The boy decided to leave.

He didn't know where he was going—not all the way home, he thought, but far enough that his grandmother couldn't find him. He walked to the other side of the house and kept walking. The boy's boots were loose on his feet. They made clopping sounds like a horse.

In a gully, where rainwater had made a steep hill, the boy discovered a soldier. He could tell the man was a soldier because of his shaved hair, which the army kept short to prevent lice. The soldier was barefoot. He sat in the shade, as if he'd been sitting there a long time. The boy didn't see signs of a campfire. He wondered whether the soldier was alone.

"Hello," the boy said.

"Hello," the soldier replied. "What happened to your hands?"

The boy looked down at his palms. The bleeding had stopped. Still he wiped them against his legs and felt fresh pain.

"I was picking weeds," he said.

"You should wear gloves for that."

The soldier hadn't moved at all. His arms were limp against his sides and his chin was raised. He had big ears—like jug handles, the boy thought. Like someone had tipped him over and poured him out.

"Do you want my boots?" the boy asked. "They don't fit."

To prove his point he lifted his right foot. He didn't need to untie the laces—his ankle came free without assistance. He placed his sock on the ground and raised his other foot, and now the empty boots stood apart from him.

The boy smiled. The soldier smiled back.

"Knotted and bowed," the soldier said. "Like a birthday present."

The boy's smile faded. Was the soldier making a joke? It was difficult to tell. What was important, the boy thought, was that he pretend it was a joke even if it wasn't.

The Trail

Once there was a boy whose bones were made from wicker. His father had been a scarecrow and his mother had been a farmer, but a long time had passed since they had been a family.

The wicker boy was walking through a forest. Some hours of daylight still remained, but the trees around him cast deep shadows. The wicker boy hoped to leave the forest by nightfall. The faster he walked, the louder he could hear himself breathing.

When he came to a curve in the trail he saw

a strange man traveling the opposite way. What made the man strange, the wicker boy thought, was that he didn't have legs. He was riding a cart pulled by a dog. The man without legs looked no more pleased to see the wicker boy than the wicker boy was pleased to see him.

"Hello," the wicker boy called by way of greeting.

"Hello," the man without legs called back.

"I'll step aside so you can pass."

The man without legs seemed relieved. His dog wore a harness that yoked him to the cart. He was only a small dog, not ideally suited for the task, but he gave the effort of a much larger animal.

The wicker boy moved to one side.

"If you don't my asking," he said, as the man without legs came closer, "how long until I reach the other side of the forest?"

"Not much longer—an hour, at most. Are there many hills that way?"

"Not many. It's mostly flat."

"That's good," the man without legs said.

As his cart approached, it nearly rolled over the wicker boy's foot. Of course, the bones in his toes were made of wood, but it still would've hurt if they'd been splintered or broken. The wicker boy winced in anticipation, but the cart passed without incident, after which the man without legs tugged on the dog's harness.

"May I offer some advice?" he asked.

"Please," the wicker boy said.

The man without legs turned himself sideways so he could face the wicker boy.

"Don't stop and don't talk to anyone," he said. "There's more than just me on this trail. Not everyone has good intentions."

The wicker boy nodded. He wanted to ask for more details—whom else he could expect to meet—but the light was fading faster than ever. The man without legs nodded back. The small dog strained against his harness and the travelers parted ways.

The wicker boy walked more quickly than before. As he walked, he considered how the man without legs might've lost the bottom half of his body—whether it had happened on the trail. But, no, the wicker boy thought, it wouldn't make sense to already have the dog, the harness, and the cart too. Probably he was born that way, similar to the wicker boy, and had made the best of his situation, also similar to the wicker boy.

Life was one dark forest after another.

The Princess

A flock of geese was migrating south. Every year they followed the same route and landed in the same fields, where they'd rest before flying again.

A farmer had become accustomed to their visits. The geese were loud and they shat everywhere. They were mean, too, hissing and flapping their wings. Every year he had less patience for their behavior.

One morning the farmer awoke at dawn.

The geese were honking, as usual, and as he

lay in his bed, listening to their noise, the farmer became more and more irritated. Finally he went outside. He didn't change his bedclothes. He didn't even look for little people as he stalked through the wet grass. He picked up a stone and threw it toward the geese, where it landed in the middle of their flock.

He'd only meant to scatter them, but the rock didn't hit the ground. Instead it struck one of the birds. The geese stopped their honking. They stepped back to create a circle and revealed a wounded gosling.

"You killed the princess!" one of them yelled.

The farmer rushed forward despite the danger to himself. While the other geese crowded around, he inspected the wounded gosling, which, he determined, wasn't dead.

The farmer breathed a sigh of relief. "I can help her," he said.

A decision was made—the princess would remain in the farmer's care while the rest of the geese traveled south. If the flock stayed in one place they would risk starvation as the weather became colder and food became scarce. But they would return the following spring. If the princess hadn't recovered by then, the other geese would hold the farmer accountable.

No sooner had the flock left than the prince learned of the situation.

He was told by his advisors that a princess was recuperating on a nearby farm—an *eligible* princess, he was informed. It didn't matter that the princess was a goose. The prince's own mother, the queen, had been a frog or a goat when she'd first met his father, the king. The prince couldn't remember which, nor could he remember the story of how she'd become human. The details of his parents' courtship always made him feel queasy.

The prince traveled to the farm with his retinue. For the farmer it was like another flock had descended, equally loud.

"How would you feel about becoming human?" the prince asked the princess.

"How would *you* feel about becoming a goose?"

"That's ridiculous," he said. "My kingdom is much bigger than yours. And I have fingers and toes—a goose doesn't have fingers and toes."

"I was only making a point."

The prince frowned. He didn't like people who "made points," geese included. They usually thought they were smarter than he.

"*My* point," he emphasized, "is that we could rule together."

"And my flock—would you send word or wait until they got back?"

But the prince was thinking about different things. He was thinking how the princess might look as a human. He assumed she'd be pretty, but would their children be human? Or would they be hatched from eggs? The answers weren't found in his parents' stories, that much he knew—just a man and a frog, or a man and a goat. A person could hear the same stories hundreds of times and never learn anything useful.

For instance, a person might think it was easy being royalty—that the prince woke up every morning and everything was perfect—but no. There were taxes to be levied, contracts to be negotiated, and a pension fund for retiring soldiers. Who'd ever heard of such a thing? It wasn't like there'd been an apprenticeship, someone telling him what to do. Not his dead dad, obviously. Not his mom.

"I've already asked your father's permission," the prince said. "He agreed. We'll be married by year's end."

The princess was surprised by this answer, as were the prince's advisors. Apparently the prince had mistaken the farmer for her father. It was unclear how he'd made this mistake. Maybe he'd thought the farmer was a goose who'd turned into a man? Regardless, no one corrected him. It would've been too embarrassing to acknowledge his gaffe.

The Three Lodgers

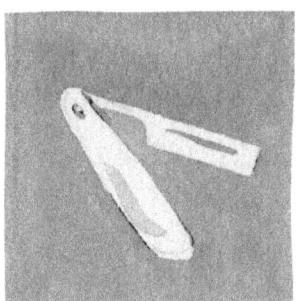

A young woman was eager to move away from home. She'd lived in the same town her entire life and had exhausted its possibilities.

Her best chance, she thought, was to find a suitor—not someone who wanted to stay in one place forever, like most of the boys her age, but someone passing through. Maybe someone who loved to dance as much as she. With this in mind the young woman took a job at the hotel, changing bedsheets and cleaning the communal toilet.

The hotel had three rooms. When all three rooms were occupied she introduced herself to the lodgers.

The first lodger was a wholesaler. He stayed to watch as the young woman made his bed, but he didn't offer to help.

"You should come with me when I leave," he said, as if he could read her mind.

The young woman smiled. Finding a suitor would be easier than she'd thought.

"Oh, yes?" she mused. "Where would we go?"

"Well, I can't bring you home to my wife—she wouldn't like that!"

The wholesaler laughed. The young woman made an effort to keep smiling as she fluffed his pillows.

"I wouldn't like that either," she agreed. "So where will I stay?"

"Somewhere close, but not too close. Do you like kids? I already have two, but I could have more."

The young woman considered his proposition. Raising the merchant's children wouldn't be so different from working in a hotel, she thought, changing *their* bedsheets and fluffing *their* pillows.

"No, thank you," she said. She smoothed a

final wrinkle before leaving his room.

She met the second lodger—a banker—later that day.

"Hello, sir," the young woman said when they passed in the hall. "Is there anything I can do to make your stay more enjoyable?"

"The toilet needs cleaning. It's like a bear took a shit in there."

The young woman was startled by his crudeness. She didn't know whether the banker was joking, but his tone lacked humor.

"I'm sorry," she said, though it was unclear what she was apologizing for. "Did you see who was responsible?"

"What do you mean? It was me."

The young woman was at a loss for words. At the same time she felt intimidated by the banker. To mock or scold him seemed like a risky idea.

"Yes, sir," she said. "I'll clean it right away."

"When you're done maybe you can join me for dinner."

The important thing wasn't to disagree, the young woman knew—it was to escape. She made a deliberately vague gesture.

"Yes, sir," she said. "First things first."

The third room was occupied by a soldier. The young woman had no desire to meet him. Her previous two encounters had been so unpleasant that she'd soured on her plan to find a suitor. However, the soldier had ordered a meal to his room. The young woman would deliver his food, after which she'd go home for the night.

"Come in, recruit," the soldier yelled when she knocked on the door. He was sitting up in bed—fully clothed, thankfully—in his jodhpurs and boots.

"Your dinner, sir. Where shall I put it?"

"Over there. And you, recruit, are you travel-ready?"

The young woman was too tired to indulge his question. Did he intend to bring her home too? That didn't seem to be the implication, she thought—there was nothing flirtatious about his posture. The soldier was sitting on his mattress like a person might straddle a horse. She wondered if he was senile, crazy, or both.

"What's your name?" he asked.

"Felan, sir."

"You'll need to shave that head, Felan. Soldiers in the king's army keep their hair short, to prevent lice. You've never seen so many lice until you've seen ten thousand men sleeping head-to-foot. They hop from bed to bed—the lice, I mean, not the men. During the day birds swoop down and catch them in their beaks. During the night it's bats. But there aren't enough birds or enough bats, so let's get it done, shall we?"

The young woman stood at the center of the room, trying to imagine what he was describing. Birds and bats! Not only that—it took a moment to grasp his broader meaning. Clearly he thought she was a recruit. She could correct him, but perhaps this was her best opportunity to leave? The king's army traveled far and wide. Soldiers were paid for their service, and she wouldn't have to suffer suitors like the wholesaler or the banker, all for the price of shaving her head.

"Yes, sir," she agreed. "Do you have a razor?"

The soldier did have a razor.

While the young woman sat at his writing desk, with a bedsheet tied around her neck, the soldier sawed at her long red hair. For someone who was either senile or crazy, he was surprisingly gentle, turning her head when necessary and never tugging.

"I can see why you keep it long," he said. "Those big ears of yours, like jug handles! But fear not—a good soldier is a good listener."

Actually she wasn't listening. The young woman was already thinking about her future.

She wouldn't go home again, she realized, neither to pack nor to say goodbye. She wouldn't work another day at the hotel. She felt excited, and in her excitement she also felt hungry, ravenously so. Looking at the plate of food she'd brought the soldier, now growing cold, she decided to eat it, every last bite. It was her plate, her food. That was her future too.

The Hermit

A hermit had been living in a cave on top of a mountain for thirty years. Only when his health declined was he willing to come down.

Recently the hermit had been sick. He'd had a fever for days—possibly three or four—and his body had ached in his muscles and joints. His stomach had refused any food. Though he'd recovered, the experience had given him a scare, because there was nobody on the mountain to care for him. What if he died, he thought, from sickness or injury? Who would even know?

The first place he visited when he left the mountain was his family home. The hermit had left behind a mother and an older brother. At the time they'd questioned his decision to leave, but, looking back, he realized he hadn't explained himself very well—something about desiring freedom. He assumed they'd be surprised to see him again, after so many years, but no one came to the door when he knocked. The house appeared to be vacant.

Only a stray dog occupied the front yard.

"Who are you?" the dog asked.

"I used to live here," the hermit said. "Where did all the people go?"

"I don't know what you mean."

The hermit tried to look through a window and was greeted by his own reflection. His hair was unkempt and he only wore enough layers to stay warm. He might not be recognizable to this mother or brother, he thought. Perhaps they'd seen him from a distance and had fled.

"Won't they feel silly," he said, "when they realize their mistake."

"Whatever you say," the dog replied.

The next place the hermit visited was the schoolhouse. There was a washroom where he could rinse his hair and a lost-and-found where he could browse for clothes. The dog walked behind him. The hermit hadn't made conversation in a long time and worried he might be out of practice.

"I've been living on a mountain," he said.

"I've been living under a porch."

"I got sick—I nearly died."

"I ate a dead bird once and threw up. It was awful."

The two lapsed into silence.

The schoolhouse was also deserted, which seemed strange to the hermit. Usually there'd be a half dozen children playing outside or seated behind their desks. In the winter there was a stove to keep the schoolhouse warm. In the summer there was an apple tree to provide shade. Children liked to climb to the highest branches and shake loose the fruit. But there was nobody present. The door was locked and overripe fruit littered the ground.

"Eat one of those and you'll get drunk," the dog said.

The hermit knew where to go next—the graveyard. He could identify the newest graves and learn who'd died, and when, and why. Obviously, he thought, something had occurred while he was away, something he couldn't see from the mountaintop. Famine? Drought? Disease? There were too many possibilities to imagine.

"Oh no," the dog said. "I ate one."

"Ate what?" the hermit asked, distracted.

"An apple."

Already, he was suffering the effects of the fermented fruit. The dog made a hacking sound like something was caught in his throat, and fell on his side. It was clear to the hermit the dog had been poisoned. He could either help or watch the dog die.

Careful not to lose a finger, he opened the dog's mouth and made the dog gag. Up came the fruit, nearly intact. In addition, the dog vomited out the hermit's mother and brother, school children of various ages, and other people whom the hermit didn't recognize, though he might've known them in his youth. Thirty years was a long time—people changed. For instance, the town's mayor. The last time the hermit had seen him he'd been a boy. Now the mayor wore a moustache on his upper lip, like a little man, as well as the mayoral sash. He blinked at the hermit, who, of course, hadn't voted for decades.

The Anniversary

An elderly husband and wife were celebrating their anniversary. The husband had arranged to experience their marriage and courtship in reverse.

Their family was happy to participate.

First their grandchildren aged backward. From the youngest to the oldest they grew smaller, their features becoming less prominent, until, one by one, their father swaddled them in blankets and delivered them to their mother, the couple's only child. With the assistance of a midwife she took them into her body. Each time, her belly became flat again and she was ready for the next child.

Once the couple's grandchildren had been unbirthed, their daughter and son-in-law spent some time with the couple before the son-in-law said goodbye, presumably to join his own parents. The couple had always liked him. They were sorry to see him go but pleased to visit with their daughter.

The elderly husband and wife were also aging in reverse. While their daughter had been preoccupied as a mother they'd reclaimed their youthful selves—their voices gaining timbre, their wrinkles fading. The elderly husband, no longer elderly, boasted a broader chest. His wife, now middle-aged, wore her hair in a braid, with nary a silver thread.

Like the couple's grandchildren, their daughter also became smaller. The couple enjoyed seeing her again as a young woman, an adolescent, and finally as a child. Grievances passed in minutes, not years. They held their daughter's hands in their clumsy palms. She sat in their laps—her perfect, little body—and they breathed in the smell of her skin.

Then it came time to swaddle her. The husband wept for joy as he brought her to his wife. There was no midwife this time—the daughter's unbirthing was a prolonged affair. Even after the wife had received her, the resulting pregnancy was uncomfortable, with frequent bouts of nausea. But everything was shorter and faster, almost too brief. Soon her round belly became flat again.

For the first time in many years the couple was alone. They felt shy toward each other. It was more challenging to nurture love than they recalled. They organized a drunken party for all their friends and became unwed. The husband-to-be made note of his wife's flaws while overlooking his own. The wife-to-be considered leaving him, once for a woman, once for another man, and once for her own solitude. They made up, argued, and forgot their reasons for being upset.

They met again for the first time.

A young man was struggling with a horse. The draft animal had stopped in the middle of the road and now refused to move, despite the young man's antics. He tried pushing, pulling, and shouting. He tried mounting the horse and dismounting the horse. He even called the animal "my darling" in a tone to suggest compromise.

A young woman witnessed this confrontation. She was amused. The more desperate the young man became, the more stoic the horse seemed to be, but the young man never resorted to violence, not even as a threat, and the young woman respected him for this. She wondered whether the horse was hungry and why the young man hadn't asked himself the same question. Perhaps he was hungry too. In her experience hunger made everything more complicated.

The young woman had a carrot. She offered half to the horse and half to the young man. Was this the anniversary they'd intended to celebrate? It hardly mattered. The young man chewed and the horse chewed, so that briefly they mirrored one another, and the young woman laughed at the similarity.

The horse smiled.

About the Author

Jamie Yourdon, a freelance editor and technical expert, received his MFA in Creative Writing from the University of Arizona. He lives in Portland, Oregon, with his two children.

Also by Jamie Yourdon:

Froelich's Ladder
The Space Between Two Deaths
Swanya

www.ingramcontent.com/pod-product-compliance
Lightning Source LLC
LaVergne TN
LVHW010156070526
838199LV00062B/4385